DESERT WAR NURSE
By David Spiller
Copyright © David Spiller

Cover art by Maria Koallas (@Koallasart on Instagram)

Also by David Spiller

Pilot Error

Girl from Dunkirk

Out of Burma

The New Messiah

5 years in India

DESERT WAR NURSE

BY

DAVID SPILLER

~ One ~

The London Hospital, September 1940

For Sara Cox it began at the London Hospital. During the early days of the second world war, hospitals in the capital were not especially hard pressed. Their main job – apart from meeting health concerns of the local population – was dealing with wounded soldiers returning from the Dunkirk fiasco. Even so nurses at the London were restricted to 45 minutes for their mid-day break. On this particular day, nurse Sara Cox grabbed her bread and dripping sandwich from the refectory and pushed open the door of the bedroom that she shared with a morose room-mate. Brenda was sprawled on her bed, face turned to the wall.

'All right, Brenda?'

'I s'pose,' came the muffled reply.

Faced by the familiar sombre surroundings – the clunky oak wardrobe, the lino floor covering – Sara changed her mind and quietly withdrew. She made for the diminutive tea-room on the 2nd floor, where staff could obtain a famously weak cuppa during most hours of the day and night. The only occupant was a girl she knew slightly, a 3rd year probationer nurse called Penny who looked up from a newspaper as Sara entered the cramped quarters.

Sara hesitated. 'Is it all right if I join you?'

'Only if you're willing to demean yourself in the company of a humble probationer.' Penny's broad smile redeemed words that might otherwise have sounded peevish.

'Don't be daft.' Sara plonked her sandwich down on Penny's table. 'Can I get you more tea?'

Penny shook her head. 'Still got some dregs here. You fetch yours.'

For a moment the woman standing behind the tea urn looked as if she might refuse to serve her, but eventually she deigned to fill a cup, allowing the tea to slop over its edges.

'I hate all these daft rules and regulations,' Sara said quietly as she slid in beside Penny. 'You know what the worst thing is?'

'You mean apart from the tea?' Penny whispered.

Sara giggled. 'It's when one of us registered nurses enters the refectory during the evening meal and the rest of you have to stand up.'

'A proper tribute to our superiors,' said Penny, giggling in turn.

Sara lowered her voice further, though nobody was listening. 'It's ridiculous. I hate it.'

'I don't mind.'

Sara turned to look directly into her companion's face. They'd never spent any time together, but she'd noticed once before Penny's very open expression; always a smile, as if in cheerful

5

mockery of the nursing experience. Her skin was very clear, like an advert for healthy living.

'Saw you in the wards yesterday,' Sara observed. 'You were taking pulses, putting on dressings.'

'Sister's letting us do that now, thank god. Better than cleaning out sputum trays. I like doing pulses. Haven't caused any deaths so far.' She picked up the copy of the *News Chronicle* that lay at her elbow. 'Here, Sara – would you like this? I've done with it.'

'Oh...' Sara felt suddenly uncomfortable. 'I don't really...'

'Irritated by the liberal bias, is that it? Do you prefer *The Times*?'

'It's not that.' The other girl's open expression encouraged her to go on. 'To tell the truth I don't really read a paper. I never have.'

'You devil.' Penny tossed the *Chronicle* into a nearby waste bin. 'They all patronise their readers, I give you that. What do your folks take at home?'

'There's only mum.' Sara felt her face redden, but she ploughed on. 'And she can't read.'

Penny looked uncomfortable and touched Sara's arm. 'Not at all?'

'She can't read or write.'

'Sara, I'm so sorry. There I go, blundering all over your private life. Please forgive me. And anyway nobody has to take a newspaper, for Christ's sake. There's always news on the radio.'

'I don't listen to that either.' Sara seemed set on burning all her boats at once. 'I like 'Housewives' choice' though.'

She could feel Penny's gaze on her. 'Can we talk more about this?' the girl said. 'I'd like to, but I've got a way of putting my foot in things. Just tell me to sod off.'

Sara gazed round the tiny space, where they were still the only incumbents. The tea-lady appeared to have fallen asleep with her head against the urn. Two nurses in uniform scurried past in the corridor. In spite of herself she felt good talking to this young girl.

'It's all right. I don't mind.'

Penny grinned. 'How on earth did we get onto this subject? What I'm thinking is that you made it through all these wretched nursing exams that I'm grappling with right now. That must've been one hell of a journey. So why not take on the more weighty stuff? Politics, for instance. After all, you can't vote unless you know what the buggers are up to. Of course the war coalition means all bets are off for the time being, but you see what I mean.'

Sara didn't see at all. And she wasn't used to a woman swearing. 'Why did you go in for nursing?' she asked. 'Look at you. You could've done all sorts.'

'You think so— like what?'

'I don't know. Join the WAAF, for instance.'

Now it was Penny's turn to look discountenanced. 'There's a problem. My dad's in France with the expeditionary force and my mother...she's not well. I can't leave her.'

'I'm sorry.'

'It's a bugger.' The smile returned, as if a switch had been pressed. 'Hey look, do you fancy a little jaunt – you and me?'

'A jaunt, blimey. Where to?'

'You know about Myra Hess?'

'What's that?'

'Myra Hess is a woman. A pianist. Since the war started she's been arranging these lunchtime concerts at the National Gallery. She's playing the piano herself on Friday and I'd thought about going. What do you reckon?'

Sara wanted to say yes but she prevaricated. 'I could get Friday afternoon off all right - we're not exactly overrun at present, are we? Thing is, Penny, I know nothing about music. You don't realise how ignorant I am.'

'All the more reason.'

The girl was irresistible. They looked at each other, and Sara nodded. 'That's arranged, then,' Penny went on. 'We can meet at the end of the street, so no-one spots you slumming it with a low-life probationer. How nice. Something I can look forward to.'

*** *** ***

On Friday the two girls met up – as Penny had suggested – a hundred yards down Whitechapel Road, and made for the National Gallery. It was immediately apparent that Penny knew her way around the centre of London, and Sara hid the fact that she didn't. They took a London bus to Fleet Street, then strolled down the Strand to Trafalgar Square. Sara found it strange to be walking around out of uniform. She'd wondered about Penny's insistence on arriving early, but was glad of it when they saw the crowd at the gallery's entrance. They stood in a queue for half an hour before coming to some wooden tables where three redoubtable females were taking the entrance fee of a shilling off concert-goers.

'Let me handle this,' Penny said, 'It was my idea,' but Sara insisted on paying her way.

'In that case I'd like to pay for afterwards,' said Penny. 'You'll see what I mean.'

Before long they were sitting amongst a throng of people in a large hall that had paintings displayed on the walls. As the lights dimmed, a dark-haired woman dressed entirely in black approached the grand piano amidst respectful applause. Before playing she made a brief announcement. Sara caught the word 'Bach'.

The music that flowed from the woman's restless fingers sounded agreeable enough, but Sara had no way of coming to terms with it. She'd heard nothing remotely similar on 'Housewives' choice'. For that matter she'd not been to the

National Gallery before, nor seen paintings like the ones displayed there.

When the concert ended, Penny was quickly on her feet. 'We're making for the door behind,' she said. 'Follow me.'

The adjoining room was a canteen, where a line of ladies stood beside more wooden tables containing tea and coffee and sandwiches. This time the queue moved swiftly.

'My shout,' said Penny.

'Penny, really...'

'It's no problem, Sara, honestly. I'm all right for cash. That's the best thing about me.'

They settled at a long table with dozens of other people, sandwiches and drinks before them. Sara hadn't tasted coffee before but she kept quiet about it.

'So what did you think?' Penny asked.

'Blimey Penny, most of that went over my head.'

Penny nodded. 'Bach takes some getting used to.'

'There was one bit that got to me. I think she said it was Mozart.'

'There you go then. Showing off your good taste already.'

A matronly figure to her right, making short work of a whole plate of sandwiches, nodded in apparent agreement.

'So you liked that Mozart too?' Sara asked Penny.

'I did. It's a Fantasia. I can't think of any piano piece that's more wonderful.'

'It sounds like you know about these things.'

'I dabble a bit on the old keys. Not on a Steinway though.'

'You do realise I can hardly understand a word you say.'

Penny laughed. 'Steinway is a posh make of piano. The poshest.'

'The woman who played it. Very black hair. Is she foreign?'

'Depends what you mean. She's English. She's also Jewish. Like me – I'm Jewish too.'

At this the matronly sandwich-scoffer gave a sharp sideways look. Penny ignored her, but Sara stared back very obviously, saying 'Yes? Can I help?'

'Don't bother about her,' Penny said, as the two girls moved from the table. 'Happens all the time.'

'It won't happen while I'm around.'

Penny leant across to kiss her companion's cheek. 'We could wander back by the river, if you're not in a hurry.'

'We have to be back for the evening shift, but yes, I'd like to.'

For as long as the sun lasted they found the river very agreeable. The pair took their time, more than once stopping to

sit on a wall and talk. It made a big contrast to the London
Hospital, where the work was physical and enclosed in
uncongenial surroundings. As they talked Sara felt an increasing
sense of pleasure in Penny's company. She also believed – and
hoped – that the pleasure was mutual.

Even so, thoughts about work soon began to predominate.
They left the Thames at London Bridge and went north towards
the hospital.

As they struck Whitechapel Road near Aldgate the sun went
behind clouds and the temperature dropped, making London's
East End look unappealing. They were a few hundred yards
from the hospital when a sudden, strident racket disturbed the
calm of the evening.

Penny stopped dead on the pavement. 'What the hell...'

'That's got to be an air raid siren,' Sara said. 'I wondered
what it would sound like. A trial run, I suppose.'

Penny's 'Maybe' sounded doubtful.

Sara started to scan the sky but as she did they heard the
grinding roar that would soon become familiar, and saw the first
dark forms of enemy aircraft disfigure the sky. At once the
street filled with people running.

'So now it's begun,' Sara said, mostly to herself. Way down
the road she saw the top of a tall building detach itself to fall on
the street below in a welter of bricks and smashed materials.
That it seemed to happen in silence – because of the

surrounding noise – left a powerful impression upon her.

Sara's immediate instinct was to shrink back under cover, but Penny pulled her into the middle of the road, shouting 'Less likely to be hit by falling masonry.'

Now incendiary bombs brought flames in their wake, and were followed by high explosives that sent buildings crashing to the ground.

'Look!' Penny was pointing wildly.

To Sara it seemed the surface of the street had developed a life of its own, until she saw that hundreds of rats were fleeing for their lives from the burning buildings. One of the creatures brushed against her shoe. She took Penny's arm.

'Come on. They're only rats. We'll be needed at work.'

But before the girls had gone any distance they had to stop again. An Indian woman was on the pavement with a son in his early teens who was bleeding profusely from a wound in his thigh. No sound came from the boy, wild-eyed in shock, but his mother screamed hysterically, waving her arms around. They could get no sense from her. Though she hated doing it, Sara gave her a single, hard slap to the face, which had an immediate effect. She put an arm around the woman, who was now crying quietly.

'We're nurses. We can help you.'

Penny laid her jacket on the pavement and they helped the boy to lie down, ripping away the torn trouser leg. Blood

13

pumped alarmingly from a jagged wound in his thigh.

'It's the femoral artery,' Sara said. 'We need a tourniquet.' She looked around briefly, then without more ado stripped off her blouse and tore from it a long stretch of material. She twisted this round the boy's thigh above the wound. Still the blood flowed, albeit more sluggishly. Penny produced a hair-brush from her bag.

'Use this.'

'Just the job.' Sara, inserted the brush handle into a knot in the material and twisted till the blood stopped. Penny ripped another piece of the blouse to secure the brush in place.

'Now the hospital.'

Sara looked around for help. People were running crazily in all directions, but there was no sign of air raid wardens or stretcher bearers. She clenched her left hand over Penny's right so that their arms formed a rudimentary sling and manoeuvred the boy onto it, while his mother supported from behind. The weird quartet began to shuffle forward.

Sara tried to shut out the pandemonium in Whitechapel Road and concentrate on reaching the hospital. Two hundred yards seemed like a mile, with their awkward burden in tow. She pressed ahead, trying to ignore the strain on her arm muscles. Penny was suffering too, though she did gaze appraisingly at her companion's upper body, naked but for the the bra.

'You look good without clothes on.'

14

Finally – 'At last', Penny muttered under her breath, they reached The London Hospital. Sara had hated the place often enough, but she now felt an obscure sense of pride seeing that here at least something was working amidst the chaos. Ambulance men unloaded two patients onto trolleys that were swiftly wheeled into the building. Half a dozen wounded people had been laid on the hospital steps, where a doctor looked them over and gave instructions to paramedics. Someone else noted particulars for the hospital's records. The first air-raid of the war, Sara thought, and the hospital's detailed planning was paying off.

They loaded their teenage burden onto a trolley and told a paramedic where to take him. The boy's mother followed, still crying quietly.

The girls rubbed their wrists and flexed aching muscles. Their clothing dripped with blood.

'Now I've seen the real thing,' Penny commented.   'And by the way, Miss Sara Cox, you are a bloody amazing nurse.'

'We did it together,' Sara murmured.

When they reported to Sister, they were ticked off for being late.

***   ***   ***

Accommodation at The London Hospital had its limitations, but three years earlier Sara had been relieved to move away from problems at home. As a form of penance, she made herself return once a month to spend a night under her mother's roof. As for a father, there wasn't one, and never had been as far as Sara was concerned.

Three days after the first German bombing raid she set out for another visit home. Sister was reluctant to release her, but Sara argued that her mother was unwell and needed attention. This was both true and untrue. Certainly her mother suffered from a depression brought on by circumstances and temperament, but this had been so for most of her adult life. On the other hand there was a particular reason for concern. Her mother worked at a factory that made armaments, part of the country's belated war effort. In the course of this job she had apparently gashed her hand badly and sustained an infection that – as Sara understood it, had refused to go away. Treatment at the factory itself had been rudimentary and her mother lacked the funds for a doctor, so the wound wouldn't heal. There was nothing unusual about this; good medical treatment was for the well off, and the poor had to fend for themselves. As Sara left The London that morning she was guiltily aware of items in her bag that shouldn't be there – a gauze dressing and some antiseptic. Should these be discovered she would doubtless be dismissed from the service in disgrace. So on passing unhindered through the hospital's main entrance and out into the bomb-ravaged street, she breathed a sigh of relief.

The capital's transport systems were still in a jam after the bombing, but Sara, used to their vagaries, negotiated the two buses needed to reach Finsbury Park.

Nearing home, she walked through the familiar seedy streets with a mixture of emotions: the pull of what was, after all, home, but also an exasperation stemming from the time she'd lived there.

Not far from the house she noticed some serious bomb damage to a group of prefabs, and quickened her step. The notion that 'home' might have suffered in the air raids hadn't occurred to her. But reaching the end of her street she saw with relief that all the terraced housing there had remained intact.

It was a Saturday and Sara hoped her mother was at home because she hadn't – couldn't have – given advance warning of the visit. She knocked on the front door, which badly needed some paint. They'd only ever had one key between them, and when both were in residence used a system that involved leaving the key upon a ledge near the entrance.

The door opened and her mother's face peered from the darkened hallway.

'Oh it's you.'

'I'm overwhelmed by the warmth of your greeting, mother.'

'Well come in then, if you're coming.'

They moved through the dining room into the cramped

kitchen, where a saucepan was bubbling on a gas ring. As usual Sara was struck by the contrast between The London Hospital – no oil painting itself – and her bleak former home: three meagre rooms up and down, an outside toilet, cold water from one sink. For an instant she visualised Penny's parental home, which she knew was in leafy Hampstead.

'Are you OK?' she asked her mother.

'I have to be, don't I.'

'I saw the bomb damage in Lorne Road. That was a close one.'

'Pity it wasn't closer. They can drop one on me any time – I'd welcome it.'

'Don't say that, mum.'

'What about where you are? Was there any trouble?'

The tone was casual, but Sara knew her mother and was touched by the implicit note of concern. She explained about the raid in Whitechapel Road. 'And what shape are you in here?' she asked. 'I can go out for some grub if you like.'

'You won't find much in the shops. Anyway, no need. I've got some soup on. There's bread.' Her mother gestured round the kitchen. 'The place is a mess, but I didn't know you were coming.'

Sara grinned. She admired women who weren't remotely house-proud. The kitchen windows were so grubby you could barely see through them. The shelf above the gas stove harboured a big pile of used match stubs that had mounted up over several weeks. Well done mother, she thought. If I ever have a home of my own, I'll follow your lead.

Unusually, her mother was wearing rubber gloves, and Sara glimpsed the edge of a bandage under one of them. She took her mother gently by the arm.

'Let me have a look at that hand.'

'It's all right, Sara. Don't fuss.'

'Let me see.'

Off came the glove, revealing a grubby and unpleasantly stained bandage. She found the kitchen scissors in their usual place and cut the material away. The burnt, suppurating flesh caused even a qualified nurse like her to suppress a gasp of alarm. She looked her mother in the eye.

'So it's all right, is it?'

'What can I do?'

'It's what *I* can do, mum. You should have called me earlier. I'm surprised you're able to work with this.'

The older woman wouldn't meet her gaze. 'Actually I've not been in recently.'

'No, I bet. It's disgraceful that they've left you like this.' She took the smuggled hospital medication from her bag. 'I need to clean up the wound. But this is going to hurt.'

19

Her mother shrugged.

'OK then.'

Sara boiled the kettle for hot water, then guided her mother to the sink and used soap and water on the injured hand. She found the bottle of Dettol in its usual place under the sink, and poured some onto the raw-looking flesh.

'Sorry about this, mum.'

She knew it would be hurting like blazes but her mother didn't make a sound, though her lips were unnaturally compressed. Meanwhile Sara took some sulphonamide tablets that she'd filched from the hospital and ground them to a powder on the kitchen table.

'What's that?'

'It's the antiseptic we use at the hospital. There are rumours of some miracle new substance on the way, but we've not seen hair or hide of it.'

Her mother sat, hand on the table, while Sara applied the powder and fixed over it a tight dressing of Vaseline gauze. Still not a murmur of discomfort.

'A model patient,' Sara said.

'You seem quite professional.'

The grudging compliment – so unusual – took Sara by surprise, but she managed to squeeze out a 'thank you'. She told her mother to stay off work for at least three weeks and to keep the hand dry.

'There's no guaranteed way of treating this,' she went on, 'But one of the hospital doctors has a system I believe in. He says it heals better if you prevent air from getting to the wound. So only take off the dressing after five days. It'll look revolting then – pus all over the place – but if you clean it with salt and water, with any luck the skin will start to grow back.'

They had the soup, together with some bread and margarine, and managed to communicate without falling out, which was not always the case. Afterwards Sara went shopping with a list of things her mother needed, only some of which proved to be available. Food shortages were widespread. There was a long queue at the butcher's, though a woman at the tail end didn't know what she was queueing for. Sara bought an extra item from the chemist's – a scent that her mother was fond of but wouldn't have splashed money on. She looked in at the greengrocer's for fruit, without luck. She called at a café called 'Bunter's' where they'd sometimes eaten together, and checked that it was open till 8pm. For old times' sake she took a walk in the park.

The brief tour of an area she'd known so well led to a mild lowering of her spirits. The landscape had been disfigured in several places by bombing, and people's morale seemed some distance from the 'Britain can take it' slogans that were already becoming common currency. There was clearly very little money around.

Back home, she invited her mother to eat at Bunter's that

21

evening, and was pleased to get an 'OK'. At 6pm they were seated opposite each other in the café's familiar surroundings, though the menu bore little resemblance to what they'd known in 'the old days'. Her mother wore a blouse Sara hadn't seen before and had dabbed on some of the new perfume. In place of the harassed and unwell person she'd seemed to be earlier, the woman opposite had rekindled elements of attractiveness from an earlier era. Perhaps even – here Sara's thoughts drifted into a forbidden zone – an aura that had drawn her father, whoever he was, into the fateful coupling that brought her own life into existence.

*** *** ***

A feature that had initially sparked Sara's interest in The London Hospital was the existence of a swimming pool deep in the bowels of the building. Nurses were allowed to use it during off-work periods, and Sara and Penny were two who did. A month after that first, devastating bombing raid they had the place to themselves during an evening break. They drifted lazily up and down the length of the pool, stopping now and then to talk. The area was dimly illuminated, but such lights as there were left patterns on the churned up water. Somewhere not far away bombs were falling on London, yet the atmosphere in the pool conferred a calming effect.

Sara turned on her back to watch her friend progress with a lazy breast-stroke. Even in the rubber bathing-cap the girls were required to wear, Penny looked good; a healthy young woman, elegant, intelligent. Now she broke off and joined Sara at the side, where they floated at rest, shoulders just touching.

'Do you like it here at the hospital?' Penny asked, out of the blue.

Sara considered. 'It's hard to say. I like doing something that's useful, despite all the unpleasantness, the pain. I can't see many other ways that my life can go.'

'Mmm.' Penny splashed her feet idly in the water. 'Have you thought about going abroad?'

'God Penny, no. I've not been further than Southend.'

'I was thinking, to work. You've heard of the QA's?'

'Just about. Though I don't know what 'QA' stands for.'

'Queen Alexandria Imperial Military Nursing Service for Women.'

'Bit of a mouthful. Correct me if I'm wrong, but we're talking about respectable middle-class girls here, aren't we? They wouldn't want me. I can't play tennis.'

Penny trilled with laughter. 'War changes everything, Sara. Always has done. These days they're interested in everyone they can get – even mongrels like you. Imagine what they'll need when the real fighting starts. You know a thousand nurses went out to France with the British Expeditionary Force.'

Sara turned in the water to look her friend in the eyes.

'You're serious, aren't you? Where are you going with this?'

Penny returned the look. 'I think you'd enjoy it, that's all.'

Out of nowhere came a tremendous crash from quite nearby. The building shook, and fragments of plaster drifted down into the water.

'As I was saying,' Penny continued without a break. 'Things would be much freer overseas. People can get up to things. You wouldn't get fined for wearing heels in a restaurant, as happened to Susan Gibbs a few weeks ago.'

'Hm.'

'And the uniform's much nicer. A lovely scarlet-trimmed cape.'

'Now you're talking,' Sara said. 'All the same. I could end up anywhere. In some hell-hole.'

'Not really. You can choose where to go.'

'You're always so well informed, Penny. I don't know how you do it. Where would *you* choose?'

'Oh well...of course it all depends where the fighting is. At present...' She thought for a moment. 'Cairo.'

'Why?'

'It's a crazy place just now. All sorts of eccentric odds and sods fetching up there. You'd have a ball.'

Sara turned to take her friend by the shoulders and kiss her face. 'This is all very interesting, but *you* can't travel, can you?'

'No, I can't. I'm going to miss you terribly when you leave.'

'You don't understand. Your friendship means a lot to me. I wouldn't leave if you have to stay.'

The double doors into the pool area broke open with a crash, and two men in overalls entered, dragging behind them a great length of hosepipe attached to a pump.

'Sorry ladies,' said one. 'We need some of your water to put out fires. Do stay put if you wish. Be careful you don't get sucked into the hose.'

The girls looked at each other.

'I think we'll call it a day,' said Sara.

*** *** ***

After the shock of that first bombing raid the German attacks continued unabated. With the docks in close proximity it was clear the East End would bear the brunt of Hitler's aggression for a while to come. Nurses at The London didn't exactly get used to it, but they knew what to expect. As time passed and there were only near misses, some of the staff perhaps came to believe in the fantasy of a 'charmed life'.

A middle-aged porter called Mr Hastings had a theory about the bombing. Penny was a fan of this man, whom she described as 'the salt of the earth'. He'd brought in a cat called 'Mr Tibbins' to tackle the endemic mouse problem at the hospital. But Sara never came to terms with the long-winded way Hastings expounded his 'views', of which there were many, and on many different subjects. It came to a head when she went up onto the roof to hang out her washing, as all the nurses did, and the porter accused her of doing so in a manner that sent messages to the German bombers. After that the two of them were never reconciled.

The London finally ran out of luck on a Friday evening around 9pm, when one of the near misses was so close it blew out the windows of the hospital's top two floors. The blast was like nothing they'd experienced before. One moment Sara was attending to bedridden patients, and a second later beams and girders came down from the roof, and the window frames on the Whitechapel Road side sliced across the ward. She saw three colleagues go down before realising that she was to be the fourth. At the same moment she saw an iron girder fall ponderously towards the prone form of a nurse, and her old adversary Mr Hastings throw himself onto the woman with a redundant pretentiousness (at least in Sara's eyes – 'What a bitch I am', she thought') in a quixotic gesture that would nevertheless lead to the deaths of both Hastings and the nurse.

Hard upon these disturbing scenes came a pain more extreme than any Sara had known. She tried to rise, then for a time knew nothing more. When she regained consciousness Sister was in the ward, giving orders to a small team, radiating a calmness none of them could emulate.

'Don't try to move, nurse,' Sister said. 'You'll be all right. Doctors are on their way. There are some big shards of glass in your back. So much for all that sticky tape they put on the windows.'

She was given water with tranquillisers, and in time the doctors came to sort her out.

Sara was actually in bed, lying very deliberately on one side, when a dreadful thought crossed her mind. She rolled off the sheets, ignoring colleagues who sought to stop her, and lurched down a flight of stairs to where Penny had been working. The scene of destruction there brought an involuntary gasp from her throat.

A nurse was sweeping debris from the floor and Sara uttered one word.

'Penny?'

The girl grimaced and pointed to a corner of the floor, concealed behind more wreckage.

Penny's ghostly form had not been moved from the spot where she'd fallen. They'd made her as comfortable as possible but the ashen skin, the blood still seeping from hastily improvised bandages, told their story. Sara knelt and took Penny's icy hand in hers. Nurses were trained not to allow facial expressions to reveal their feelings, but neither girl tried to dissemble.

'Get out of here, Sara,' Penny whispered, 'The way we talked about. Go abroad'.

Her eyes closed.

Sara had become accustomed to death, especially in wartime, but this was different. There were no tears – Sara was beyond that – but she was never to forget that in her last moments Penny had been thinking about someone else's future. *Her* future. That moment in the smashed ward was to exert a big influence upon her immediate future, and on the years beyond.

***   ***   ***

The weeks before Sara set off for North Africa were a chaotic time for a girl who had 'never been further than Southend'. Matron at The London disapproved of the move, but the demand for nurses overseas was too insistent to be resisted.

Sara's mother was a different story, and she remained baffled by her daughter's desire to travel. Her attitude cast a cloud over the last weeks in Britain.

Sara made a final visit to Finsbury Park a few days before her departure. She felt guilty as hell, but was set on going. She found her mother in the kitchen doing the washing up, and was relieved to note the injured hand healing well.

'So this is it then,' her mother said.

'I know.' Sara managed an awkward hug. 'It feels strange.'

'But you're still determined to go.'

'I must try it. I hope you'll be all right here.'

'Oh you don't have to worry about me.'

'I was thinking, there is one thing...something that could help you.'

'What! What do you mean by that?'

'Don't fly off the handle mum, but...' She took the plunge. 'There's a woman called Mrs Parsons. Lives just round the corner.'

'I know who you mean. Hoity toity type. Gives herself airs.'

'The thing is...she's very literate.'

'What does that mean?'

'She's good at reading. And writing. And she teaches people who want to learn. She can teach you if you want.'

'So that's it.' Her mother threw the tea towel down. 'You're ashamed of me, aren't you.' The instant response was typical. 'No, I'm too old. It's too late.'

'I'm not ashamed, mum.' Sara was on the verge of tears. 'I love you. I admire you.'

'And you can leave off the soft soap.'

'It would make such a difference for your life.' She grasped her mother's shoulders in an unfamiliar gesture. 'Please try it. I'll be earning a bit more now, so I can cover the cost. I'll make a standing order to Mrs Parsons before I go. *Please*, mum.'

'Oh all right then, I'll give it a try.'

The abrupt change from defiance to acquiescence was also familiar. Now Sara breathed a sigh of relief and settled down to some serious crying. She felt her mother's arms around her.

'Come on love, we'll meet again eventually. It's not the end of the world.'

~ Two ~

Round Africa by ship, November 1940

In her ignorance Sara had assumed she would travel to Egypt via the Mediterranean. The reality was very different. The U-boat dangers to Allied shipping in the Med meant reaching north Africa by a circuitous way. In November 1940 she sailed from Southampton in the converted liner Cameronia. The route was to be down the western coast of Africa to round the Cape of Good Hope, then northwards up the eastern coast. Finally up the Red Sea and through the Suez Canal.

To Sara the Cameronia seemed an enormous vessel. An information leaflet told her it could accommodate 290 passengers in cabin class and a further 400 in tourist. On this trip the ship was far from full, but there were plenty of soldiers going to join their units, some nurses, and a variety of ordinary citizens.

As it happened Sara was never able properly to participate in the social life of the journey. Unusually for a grown woman of 23 she'd never been on any kind of ship before. As the Cameronia emerged from Southampton harbour her stomach instantly objected to the rhythm of the engines; and when they moved into open water the irregular swell of the waves undermined her totally. She ran to her cabin and threw up her lunch into the sink.

Sinking back onto one of the bunks, her first thought was

31

relief that she had the cabin to herself. But almost at once the door opened and a young woman blundered in dragging a suitcase.

'Sorry I'm late,' said the new entrant. 'Too bonkers to explain. I'm Gina.'

Sara introduced herself, then made another rush for the sink, flinging a 'Sorry' over her shoulder.

'Seasick?' said the girl.

Sara nodded. 'It must be that. I've never sailed before.'

A bit later she threw up again, just making it to the sink in time.

'Gawd, girl.' The newcomer stood over her. 'And you ain't seen nothing yet. This is just a choppy sea. Wait till we get to the Cape of Good Hope.'

'Is that bad?'

'Famous for it. You'll be spewing your guts up.'

As Sara made a third dash for the sink the new girl jumped from her bunk muttering 'That does it', and left the cabin in a hurry.

'Oh god,' Sara murmured, prostrate on her bunk, 'What have I done?' At that moment her most fervent wish was to have stayed at The London Hospital, with all its tiresome little ways. And she regretted already the appearance of this cabin mate who, she decided, was not at all the sort of person she could get on with. Something about Gina's appearance grated – maybe the ridiculous polka dot dress that didn't go with those clunky shoes. And the coarse way she talked! What was that about? 'Am I turning into my mother?' Sara wondered, denouncing someone for 'not speaking nicely' (when her mother had been dragged up in the gutter, for god's sake). As for the girl's blunt manner, no social niceties to speak of...

The cabin door opened and Gina barged back in, this time carrying a china dish. She crossed to Sara's bunk and handed it over.

'Here. Got this from the kitchens for you to puke in. So you needn't be up and down to the sink. They said you can keep it till the lurgy goes away. Gawd darlin', you're a sight. Your face is red as a lobster.'

Sara knew her face was burning; it burnt from shame at her ungrateful reaction, when the new girl had been so helpful.

'I'm really sorry,' she said.

'Why's that then?'

'I was rude to you.'

'You were barfing your guts up.' Gina moved across to the port-hole. 'OK if I open this? Some fresh air may help.'

'Of course. I'm so sorry.'

For a moment she felt better, as sea air filled the cabin. Gina was peering out. 'Can't see nuffing but water now. S'pose it'll be like this for weeks. You goin' all the way?'

'All the way?'

'To Egypt?'

'Oh...yes, that's right. I'm a nurse. I'll be working in a Cairo hospital.' She retched delicately into the bowl, wiping her mouth with a handkerchief. 'Thanks so much for the dish. Why are *you* making this trip?'

'You won't believe it – I'll be interpreting.'

'Sorry?'

'Told you. Yeah, there's a whole load of Italians out there in the desert, and I speak their language.'

'I thought it was Germans.'

'Not just now, or so they told us.' She broke off as the ship's engines raised their game and Sara's stomach responded. 'And quite a lot of them Italians is prisoners. They can't wait to surrender, you know. They ain't made for fighting.'

It was hard to think, but Sara felt she should make the effort. 'I was only taught French at school, and then badly.'

'Oh yeah, me too. But I'm Italian, sort of. Second generation. Me mum's Italian, married to an Englishman. They run a greengrocer's shop in north London. She brought me up speaking her native language. Thought it might come in handy – and now it has.'

'But weren't the Army worried about...I mean...'

'You mean, did they think I'd go over to the enemy.' Gina grinned. 'Nah. None of that. 'Ad to go through lots of tests, mind you, but I convinced 'em in the end. I'll get the truth out've the little buggers, see if I don't, even if I 'ave to grab 'em by the you know whats. Or praps I'll sweet-talk it out've 'em. I could do it, too.'

'Well I never.' Sara felt surprised and a little shocked.

'I know what you're thinking, you poor girl. I'll shut up now and give you a break. We'll 'ave a good gossip later, eh?'

***   ***   ***

Sara's sickness did not lift, as sea-sickness was supposed to do. For days she dozed on and off, but always woke to more action with the sick bowl, and mopping her face with handkerchiefs. It amazed her that anything remained in her belly to bring up. She'd read somewhere that sea-sickness was like being in love: you felt terrible and thought you were going to die, then when it was over you wondered what the fuss was about. Sara had never been in love, and after this experience she was loathe to try it.

Despite earlier misgivings, Gina was a considerate room-mate, quiet and helpful. She forbore from smoking in the room and spent hours staring through the port-hole, 'looking at bugger all', as she put it. She brought soup from the dining

35

room – 'You must eat somefing, darlin' – and took it back again. One morning Sara woke to find that the half-dozen handkerchiefs she'd used to mop up spew had been washed and spread out to dry. After five days Gina fetched the ship's doctor to their cabin, but the man had little to offer beyond 'Worst case of sea-sickness I've ever seen,' and a suggestion to go up on deck. Sara tried this, leaning on Gina's arm. For a time the fresh air was helpful, and she was mildly encouraged to see other sufferers in the throes, not least a major in uniform who marched smartly to the ship's guard-rail and barked out his puke four times at precise military intervals. She noted that quite a few men, of all shapes and sizes, greeted Gina enthusiastically, and she recollected that on one – or was it two – evenings, surely well into the small hours, as she herself tossed groggily in bilious misery, Gina's bunk had been empty.

Halfway through the second week the intimacy between the two girls deepened. It was an evening when Sara despaired of ever feeling well again. Gina had perched on the bunk to mop her brow using a damp cloth infused with an agreeable fragrance.

'It's not fair,' Gina said quietly, 'That you should have to put up with this.'

'I'm lucky you were here. You've made it bearable.'

'Do you sometimes wish you'd stayed at home?'

Sara considered. 'Sometimes, maybe...but no, no, I don't. Once you decide, you have to take what comes. The friend who persuaded me to come...she died.'

36

'Was she nice?'

'She was very nice.'

'Why *did* you come?' Gina asked. 'Was it the usual reason?'

After a moment Sara asked 'Um...what *is* the usual reason?'

'To bag a husband, of course.'

In her surprise, Sara sat up in the bunk. 'No – of course not. Never gave that a thought.' Then 'Was that why *you* agreed to come out here?'

Gina laughed. 'Course it was. That's why loads of girls come out. What did you think?'

'I don't know. Can't you find a husband in London?'

Gina snorted. 'There's still some men left in London, of course, but not...'

'What?'

'Well for instance, there's an older bloke in our street who works at the fish and chip shop. 'E's bin on my tail for months. Does that answer your question?'

Before Sara could reply the plangent blast of a ship's hooter penetrated the cabin and then, louder, an answering call from the Cameronia. Without needing to move both girls saw, through the open port-hole, a large vessel with lights blazing drift across their line of vision. The sight of it affected Sara strangely. Here was a familiar expression made manifest – two

ships passing in the night in the middle of the Indian Ocean –
with all its connotations of distant lands, loneliness, an
uncertain future. All at once she felt painfully alienated from
her old life in Finsbury Park and The London Hospital, and all
that it had represented.

'You know, I've no experience of men,' she told Gina. 'I'm an
only child, never knew my father. I mean, I've worked with men
but I don't know anything about them. Never been out with
one, for instance – wouldn't know what to do.'

Gina snorted again. 'Oh, they'll know what to do all right.
You 'ave to watch it, though. Some of 'em need careful
handling. But I dunno, can't imagine life without the buggers. I
mean, what would I do in my spare time?'

Sara shrugged. 'I don't know. Read a book?'

'It's a funny thing,' Gina said. 'I've never read a book. Does
that sound terrible?'

'Blimey, Gina, there's worse things than that. Like me never
going out with a man. It's ridiculous, isn't it. Perhaps I'll break
my duck in Cairo. What d'you think?'

Gina shrieked with laughter. 'Darlin', Cairo will be *bursting*
with blokes desperate to meet women. All they'll 'ave seen for
months is sand and tanks and the back ends of camels. A nice
young girl like you, she's gonna be a very scarce bit of
merchandise. Don't you worry, I'll take you under my wing.
Officers only, of course. Other ranks ain't allowed in the big
hotels or the night-clubs. Fing is wiv men so far from home,

38

they go off the rails a bit. Like they miss their mothers, fink they're gonna die, see a cute young woman and believe they're in love – and who's gonna tell 'em different, eh? Gawd, darlin', it's all ahead of you. I'll sort you out a good one to start off wiv.'

'Let's hope I don't throw up all over him,' said Sara, reaching for the bowl.

*** *** ***

For some reason – which may or may not have been associated with geography – Sara's health improved as soon as the Cameronia sailed into the Red Sea. This turn for the better needed time before it took any physical effect, since she'd barely eaten properly for weeks. The flesh hung from her arms and her features had a gaunt aspect. In the dining room she forced down food from the unexciting wartime menu, and by degrees the colour returned to her cheeks.

` Two or three times a day she went on deck, with Gina for support. They sat in deckchairs, protected by umbrellas from the sun (if it shone). Before leaving London Sara had checked out the Red Sea in an old school atlas, and noted how it was represented by a narrow gap between the great land masses of Africa and Arabia. So her first reaction was surprise at the breadth of the 'sea' – 190 miles at its widest point, according to a male acquaintance of Gina's, of whom there were a surprisingly large number on board. Still, the Cameronia followed a course close to the Saudi Arabia coast. The contrast between the arid desert and the brilliant turquoise water struck Sara forcibly, and she remarked on it to Gina.

'Yes darlin', and Hisham says to take a good look at the coral reefs what runs along the water's edge.'

'Who's Hisham?'

'Oh just a bloke I got talkin' to.'

'Hm. Actually I've already seen some of that coral stuff. Of course it's very interesting and all that, but I thought there was something obscene about it. That coral seems to be alive.'

'Yes, because it is.'

'I see. Was that Hisham again?'

'No, that was Ahmed.'

They both laughed.

A little later, Ahmed turned up. Sara judged him to be some 40 years old. He had an agreeable expression and spoke serviceable English.

'Is it too much hot for you on deck?' He asked Sara, and even sounded interested in her reply.

'A bit, but this wind cools me down.'

'Yes, of course. Always wind in the Red Sea.'

The man seemed to know what he was talking about, so she

asked 'Do people ever swim in the water?'

'Well now...'

There followed a question and answer session about swimming. According to Ahmed the Red Sea was one of the saltiest stretches of sea-water on earth, so staying afloat was not a problem. And there were wonderful things to see down there, like mountains of coral rising from the sea bed, shipwrecks galore. The water also teemed with life -- sharks, which were 'not usually' dangerous, but also sting-rays, Moray eels. Quite quickly, the girls put aside the notion of swimming.

At length Ahmed had risen to his feet and bowed. 'Ladies. Time for lunch.'

'He seems like a good man,' Sara said, as the stolid figure moved away.

'He is,' said Gina, 'And there's something I want to tell you about him.'

Now Sara learnt that Ahmed owned a flat in central Cairo, and had offered to rent it to Gina.   'You could come and stay with me during your time off or whenever you want,' Gina said, 'If you like.' And despite their obvious differences in character, Sara knew at once that she *would* like to see more of this friendly force from another planet; that she would enjoy her company and along the way learn some things that she needed to learn. There was just one thing. If Ahmed saw the arrangement as a cosy little love nest for himself and Gina, no way did Sara want a part of that. Her friend immediately poured cold water on the notion.

'Gawd no, darlin', you ain't seen his wife.'

'What – do you think she's a bit of a dragon?'

'Don't think so, but what she is is drop dead beautiful. Ahmed's not going to stray, take it from me. In any case he's not that sort of bloke. He's very straight. You can always tell, can't you.'

'Can you?'

Gina leaned across to kiss her friend. 'Yes, you can. I'm so glad we'll be staying in touch. Garden City, here I come.'

The Cameronia sailed on through the vivid blue waters, past miles and miles of desolate waste-land. The world seemed to be at peace; no bombers threatening from the sky, no U-boats lurking in these waters.

Gazing ahead, feeling at last the unfamiliar promptings of hunger, Sara felt she should make the most of this journey, or what remained of it, because whatever lay in store for them was going to be very different.

*** *** ***

The girls were so accustomed to passing through broad expanses of water that the narrow confines of the Suez Canal took some getting used to. But almost before they knew it they'd reached their destination, which meant Egypt and the end of travelling – except, as they were to find, not straight away. In the confused melee encountered after disembarkation, the government-sponsored people due in Cairo were driven on the back of a lorry to a dismal location a few kilometres away, off-loaded into a series of tents, and told to await transport that would turn up within 24 hours (in reality, 36). The brief journey familiarised the girls with the desert's worst features, including the way sand insinuated itself into every nook and cranny, including places Sara was unwilling to discuss. The camp beds were fitted with nets to keep out the flies and mosquitoes that plagued the girls' waking moments. Sara and Gina, sharing a tent with two others, came across a scorpion emerging from the tattered floor covering. When they used the very basic latrine facilities at night, girls learnt to take along a stick to discourage the rats.

'This ain't no Garden City darlin', is it,' said Gina, disillusioned but not down-hearted.

There was relief when a batch of coaches eventually arrived to take the women to locations in and around Cairo. An unshaven Egyptian recited names from a long list and directed girls to relevant coaches. Now came an unwelcome surprise because Sara and Gina were in different vehicles and had just a few moments to say goodbye. The Italian was the better prepared. She thrust into Sara's hand a scrap of paper bearing a

Cairo address and clasped her in a fierce embrace.

'Come and stay in Garden City whenever you like, darlin'. I'll leave instructions with the bloke at the door sayin' you're to be let in if I'm not around. See you soon, eh?'

'You've been wonderful to me.' Sara felt quite tearful. 'I'll miss you.'

'Don't be daft. You're comin' to see me, remember.'

Sara shoved her out-sized bag of possessions into the luggage space above the vehicle's wheels, then climbed inside and fell onto one of the hard wooden seats. None of the other girls sat next to her. Once under-way she stared glumly through the filthy windows at unchanging scenes of desert scrub and more scrub. The abrupt separation from the warm-hearted Italian had been a shock to her system.

Sara's next conscious moment was feeling the driver's rough hand on her shoulder. In pidgin English he told her she'd arrived. She lumbered from the bus and found her possessions on the ground, next to a middle-aged woman in a hospital uniform. The sun beat down on a desolate stretch of land. A ramshackle building was in the background.

'Where am I?' said Sara, only half-awake.

'This is the British General Hospital, Helmieh.'

'Helmieh?'

Helmieh, Cairo.'

Cairo! But...' Sara recalled the few photographs she'd seen of Cairo, a city teeming with vehicles and people. 'But there's nothing here.'

The woman laughed. 'I see you are not impressed by our little community. The main city is a dozen kilometres away. Helmieh is...well, it's mainly the hospital. Come – I will show you your tent.'

After her previous night the word 'tent' gave Sara pause. But when her companion – an Indonesian lady called Rose – indicated the place, her misgivings evaporated. For a start the new tent, which she was to share with Rose, was spotless. A clean tarpaulin covered the ground, and beside each of the two camp beds was a colourful rug. Mosquito nets were in place. The remaining furniture was a canvas wash-stand and an oil heater. And in this place water seemed to be freely available, unlike the previous dump where each girl had been allowed two pints per 24 hours, to cover both drinking and washing needs.

If it wasn't what Sara was accustomed to, tent life now seemed an acceptable alternative, in a war-torn country different from anything she'd known. As she sat on the camp bed collecting her thoughts, Penny's words came to her ears: 'I think you'd enjoy it.'

~ Three ~

British General Hospital, Helmieh, November 1940

After the travails of her journey to Cairo, Sara found that she took to the work at Helmieh with relief. She believed herself to be a capable nurse, and the familiar routines came naturally. Of course they were discharged in very different circumstances to those in the UK. The London Hospital had mostly dealt with civilian injuries sustained in the blitz, whereas Helmieh was about soldiers wounded in action. On her very first morning Sara dealt with a young soldier whose skin was flayed from his arms by shrapnel from a Stuka bomber. There were burns sustained by men trapped in damaged tanks, and less commonly burning aircraft. There were multiple bullet wounds when men had been pinned down by machine-gun fire. Yet more horrible wounds occurred when men had stepped on land-mines. And the staff dealt every week with amputations.

At Helmieh many such injuries came to them via a field hospital, where medics had initially tackled problems on the spot. Sara wondered what it would be like to work in such circumstances, within earshot of the battle, making life or death decisions on the spur of the moment. But then even in Helmieh the pressured wartime existence ensured that nurses did more than they usually would – taking short cuts, making minor decisions that would normally be left to doctors.

As week followed week Sara began to realise that she flourished in this environment; that the English matron in Helmieh approved of her work, and had even begun to put difficult cases her way. Despite her humble beginnings in Finsbury, where a sense of inferiority came naturally, she sensed herself developing in double-quick time. She understood that her body could respond to the demands made upon it. There was tiredness, of course, but never to the point of exhaustion. She was four inches short of six feet, and her long legs pounded Helmieh's stairways with no sense of strain.

One thing that did revive her lowly self-esteem was an ignorance about the war. She'd very little idea what was going on out there. She remembered how Gina had had to tell her they were fighting Italians in the desert, and not Germans as she'd supposed. Did it *matter*, as she struggled to save a British soldier's life, that she didn't know why he was in Egypt (or indeed that the Egyptians might prefer him to go back home). Did it *matter* whether the man belonged to a platoon or a company or whatever other damn formation the army had dreamt up? She was beginning to feel her ignorance about such matters.

During those early weeks in Helmieh Sara's attention was absorbed by the demands of a new job – the routines of a different hospital, the medical challenges thrown up by an army at war, the novelties of living under canvas. It was Rose, the Indonesian nurse, who raised the subject of Cairo. Apart from sharing Sara's tent, Rose had been entrusted with smoothing the new girl's path in unfamiliar surroundings, a task that she carried out with tact and understanding.

'I don't think you've been into Cairo yet, have you?' Rose said one evening as they were preparing for bed.

'Not so far,' Sara admitted. 'What about you, Rose – when did you last go in?'

'I sometimes go, of course, but that's different. I'm a middle-aged woman.'

'Middle-aged! Don't be daft.'

'The thing is, there's going to be a big party on Saturday at the Turf Club. Wavell's pushing the boat out.'

'Who's Wavell?'

Rose smiled. 'General Sir Archibald Wavell. Commander-in-Chief of British forces in the Middle East.'

'Oh! Sorry. That sounds important.'

'You could say that. The point is, Sara, the military are short of female company these days. All their dependants were sent home from Egypt in August. So they'll be looking for some attractive young women to decorate the Turf Club on Saturday.'

'Will you be going?'

Rose smiled gnomically. 'You know Dr Knight, I'm sure.'

'Dr Knight! Oh I've worked with him of course. He's the main man here in the hospital, isn't he?'

'He's the senior physician, yes. He thinks highly of your work and...on the social side...well, he'd be happy to escort you to the Turf Club bash – if you wanted to go.'

'I see,' said Sara, not seeing at all. She was genuinely puzzled. 'Then why doesn't he ask me?'

'Mm. In the first place, he's quite shy about that sort of thing.'

'You know, Rose, I don't get this. He's very senior and I'm very junior. And we're never going to...I mean we get on fine at work, but socially...'

'I know dear. Look, it's not something that would ever become embarrassing. He'd take you there and bring you back, introduce you to all the right people – he's a nice man. He likes to be seen with an attractive young woman because it puts observers off the scent. D'you see what I mean?'

Sara realised she was standing there with her mouth open and shut it abruptly. 'I'm sorry, I'm a bit of an innocent in these matters.'

'That's all right. Do you have a party dress?'

'I've got one in my kit. And only one.'

'That's fine, my sweet. The girls only wear one at a time for these events. So I'll tell him you'd like to go, shall I? I'm sure you'd find it interesting.'

***　***　***

The evening at the Turf Club happened just as Rose had predicted. A smartly dressed Dr Knight materialised outside Sara's tent at exactly the time arranged. She emerged in her party dress, feeling almost naked after shedding the heavy QA's uniform, and they settled into a chauffeur-driven car. Sara couldn't remember when she'd last been in one. The Turf Club was in Adley Pasha Street in an area that her companion described as 'Cairo's West End'. On a normal day, he told her, the club was not only exclusively British, but exclusively male. The portentous architecture and the genteel atmosphere within was what Sara imagined a gentleman's club in Mayfair to be like. However on this night the place was awash with khaki uniforms.

Dr Knight was meticulous about introducing Sara to people, and supervised her assault upon some tables of food that had her eyes popping. They'd been there an hour before the doctor introduced her to an officer he said would 'look after you', and finally left her side.

Lieutenant Harness was a Scotsman, whom she judged to be in his early 30s. They chose some more food and he insisted on pouring her a drink, whereupon they retired to a table in the corner. The lieutenant was attentive and Sara, inexperienced as she was, saw at once that those attentions were of a different order to Dr Knight's; Harness moved in closer, spoke more

50

intimately, caught her eye more often.

'Dr Knight said you were a lieutenant,' Sara told him. 'I don't know what that means.'

'How could you,' Harness said reasonably. 'It means I command a platoon in B company.'

They looked at each other, then both laughed. 'Sorry' Harness conceded. 'We're so used to these expressions – they signify damn all if you're not in uniform. It just means I'm in charge of a bunch of chaps who I try to keep happy. And keep alive, if possible.'

They talked about trivial things for a while. Sara reckoned the lieutenant a decent type, if not somebody she'd normally have spent time with. He seemed to like her, so she decided to pump him for information. She'd downed two drinks for the first time in years, which had loosened her tongue.

'So this enormous party,' she said, waving her glass so that wine splashed out. 'What's the idea of it?'

'You don't think soldiers should be allowed to enjoy themselves?' he countered.

'Of course, but is this *normal*?'

'No, you're quite right, it is a bit unusual. The actual fighting...' He broke off to scrutinise her keenly. 'Do you get news about that in the hospital?'

Sara shook her head. 'We just get wounded soldiers.'

He gave a snort that wasn't exactly a laugh. 'That's news of a sort, I suppose. To tell the truth, things haven't been brilliant recently. There are far too many Italians out there in the desert.'

'Yes, but...'

'But what, Sara?'

'Look I don't know – of course I don't – but I've got this Italian friend who's come out to interview captured Italian soldiers. She says they're hopeless at fighting. They just want to be taken prisoner.'

He grinned. 'True enough, but there are so many of 'em. Something like a quarter of a million.'

'Wow! And how many have we got to go up against them?'

'I'm not allowed to tell you that, but a hell of a lot less. And that's not all. The Iti's bombed Cairo in October. I expect you heard.'

'No, I hadn't arrived then.'

'And there's a German officer coming out next month. Chap called Rommel. He's meant to be hot stuff. He'll shake the buggers up, excuse my French. Anyway...' He jumped up. 'Come on, I'll introduce you to Wavell.'

'Wavell! What – the big boss.' Sara shrank back in her seat. 'No, no, no, he won't want to meet me.'

'Rather you than all these boring men in khaki. Come on.'

He pulled her, still protesting, off the chair. In a few moments she was approaching a group of officers standing with a burly, unsmiling figure at their centre. Harness went effortlessly forward and said 'Sir, I'd like to introduce Miss Sara Cox. She's a nurse at the hospital.'

Wavell took her hand. 'It's good to meet you.' Sara backed off, waiting for more, but nothing came.' The other officers grinned, again without speaking.

Now a woman appeared from somewhere and said 'Hello dear, I'm the wife. It's very good to have you here.'

They stood in silence for a couple of minutes before Harness clicked his heels, uttered a brisk 'Sir', and withdrew, tugging Sara with him. Almost at once he turned to face her.

'Well – what did you think?'

Sara stared at him, baffled. 'Are you kidding? What could I think? He didn't *say* anything.'

'I know. It's always like that. His silences are famous. His wife's nice – that was her who spoke to you afterwards – but she's not really suited to the entertaining role either.'

'Even so...' Sara thought back to Wavell's stern, monolithic figure. 'There was something about him, I couldn't say what exactly.'

'So you noticed it too.'

'What do you mean? Noticed *what*? What do *you* think of

him?'

'I admire him enormously. I revere the man. If he ordered me to march backwards through a minefield I'd do it.'

'I see.' She glanced back at the clump of officers, still standing silently together. 'D'you think others feel the same way?'

'I don't know anyone who doesn't.' He took her arm. 'Except for the powers that be. Plenty of rumours about them. I just pray the stories are wrong.'

'Powers that be! What powers are they? What are you talking about?'

He turned towards her, speaking in a low voice. 'I'm sorry – I shouldn't have said that. Please don't repeat it to anyone. I mean it.'

'How can I repeat it – you haven't told me anything.'

'That's all right then.'

Later Dr Knight returned, along with some other people, and they all stood in a group saying their 'goodbyes' prior to departure. This was the moment when Harness asked Sara if he could take her to dinner one evening at Shepheard's Hotel. She was caught by surprise and found it hard to reply. He'd been decent company but she didn't want to feel beholden to a man she scarcely knew. At the same time a trip to the celebrated Shepheard's was an appealing prospect. She accepted, still unsure about it.

Harness had made no secret of his invitation, and a rather loud woman in the group jogged Sara's elbow.

'That's right, dear – accept every damn invitation you get. Play your cards right and you'll never have to buy your own dinner again.'

The next day, thinking about her conversation with Harness, Sara wondered if he'd been hinting that Wavell was about to be sacked by Winston Churchill. Then she dismissed the idea as utter rubbish.

***   ***   ***

The evening at Shepheard's was an eye-opener for a young woman straight out of Finsbury Park. She'd not heard of the hotel herself, but it seemed everyone else had. It was situated just north of Garden City, where Gina lived in Ahmed's flat. The hotel had a renowned terrace, where you could sit to people-watch, and inside was the 'Moorish Hall' where dozens of guests sat around small tables. The building's monolithic structure meant Sara never did feel very comfortable there. Perhaps that was also down to the rule that women were not allowed into the famous 'Long Bar'. In fact, as she came to realise, Anglo-Egyptian society revelled in excluding people from as many places as possible; for instance females weren't allowed alone into the poshest hotels, and 'other ranks' soldiers were banned from just about everywhere.

That first evening was the start of Sara becoming familiar with a variety of fashionable watering-holes. At the same time as she was developing an impressive reputation at the hospital, she became a magnet for social invitations from single men. In her view this was surprising, since she always 'kept herself to herself' (in her mother's phrase), generally ending evenings out with a chaste kiss on the cheek of her companion. Still the invitations kept coming. She consorted with men who were interesting to know, and with a few who weren't. She learnt more about the progress of the war, whilst realising how much more she had to know. She learnt how to behave after two glasses of wine and how to decline a third. After a few months in Helmieh she even bought herself a second evening dress.

Given a day or two off-duty, Sara would usually stay with Gina in the Garden City flat. Gina's social life, predictably more hectic than her own, leant towards a taste for British Army officers. The first time Sara turned up at the flat, late one evening, a Lieutenant was 'just leaving'. The second time a Captain was on the premises. A few weeks later a Major was given his marching orders when Sara arrived. Despite her protests, she always got Gina's full attention during these visits. The pair of them would talk freely over a scratch lunch – Gina turning out to be an excellent cook – before going out on the town later. Unlike Sara, her friend did not technically have officer rank, meaning that some of the most appealing places were out of bounds (exclusions again). But Cairo's two branches of Groppi's – the the most famous cafés in town – would take all-comers, and the girls frequently repaired to them despite the pricey menus.

***   ***   ***

During the six months following her arrival at Cairo, Sara measured Britain's progress in the war by the number of casualties sent to Helmieh from field stations in the desert. But she also made an effort to follow events from the unreliable reports that filtered in from the battle front. What seemed incontrovertible was that a general called O'Connor – a new name to Sara – had in ten weeks urged his troops 500 miles westwards, subjugated places called Sidi Barrani, Bardia and Tobruk, and captured 130,000 Italian prisoners (swelling Gina's workload, Sara reflected with a smile). This purple period ended when O'Connor, in April 1941, was unluckily captured. By then the German commander Rommel had arrived in Tripoli and the war proceeded in a very different manner.

It was at this time, when morale in the British community had sunk to a low ebb, that Sara experienced an evening out which deflected her professional life into a surprising direction. She'd been invited by a man she barely knew – a Captain Bill Henderson – to have dinner in the restaurant-cum-dance hall on the roof of the Continental Hotel. An hour in Henderson's company was enough for her to know the evening was going to be tiresome, always a hazard for girls who were wined and dined by different escorts. Henderson was louder than most of his kind, and not for the first time Sara wished British officers would behave themselves when in contact with Egyptians.

She'd grown to dislike their habit of calling local people 'wogs', which they did openly, within hearing of the person concerned or even when addressing them directly. This kind of bumptiousness seemed to be peculiarly British. An American lawyer she met at Shepheard's had been astonished by it, and he wasn't alone. Rose once told her that the officer wards were the most unpopular in Helmieh.

Now in the Continental, as Sara glanced over at the bar, she saw the Egyptian barman go to pick up an ice-box, and a British officer arrogantly wrestle it from his grasp. Sara turned her face away in embarrassment. Beside her Henderson was already bellowing at a gauzily dressed blond woman who'd come on stage to introduce the cabaret. Sara could barely hear a word above the taunts from ranting Brits. As it happened the cabaret wasn't one of the best. A troupe of acrobats slipped up in several of their manoeuvres and one of them fell into the audience, upsetting some drinks. Then when a scantily dressed girl wrestled with a boa constrictor the snake almost got away from her, sparking panic in the front row of onlookers. Sara was resigned, feeling that an evening which had started so badly could only get worse. After the cabaret Henderson danced with her once, for form's sake, but he was clearly more interested in one of the Hungarian dancing girls, who were renowned for responding to male overtures. Sara was happy to let him go. She paused uncertainly when a personable, dark-skinned man smiled in her direction, but English girls did not consort with Egyptians and he quickly took the hint. At which point she was invited to dance by another Brit, a tall fellow with a quieter demeanour than the average officer. She had the curious

58

impression he'd been waiting for a chance to speak to her. He was a hopeless dancer and they called it a day after he trod on her toes a second time. All the same he lingered on the edge of the dance floor.

'I believe you're a nurse at Helmieh,' he told her.

'That's right.' She was astonished. 'How on earth do you know that?'

'Your reputation precedes you. Look, do you think we could sit and talk for a bit?'

She looked around, but Henderson had sloped off with the Hungarian. 'If you like,' she agreed. They settled at a table in the corner, Sara declining the offer of a drink. Most unusually her companion, who called himself 'Paddy', wanted to talk about her work. She described the kind of injuries she dealt with.

'Do you ever have to tackle stuff on your own?' he asked.

An odd question, Sara thought, but she did her best to respond. 'The hospital's short of doctors, so I sometimes do more than nurses would usually. I think they trust me. I hope so, anyway.'

'I'm sure. Would you say you're a self-sufficient person?'

'What is this? It sounds like a job interview.'

'Sorry. I'm just interested in how you girls manage.' Notwithstanding this reply, she remained puzzled by his conduct. He had a quiet seriousness that was rare in the men she met. She wasn't attracted to him, but felt he'd be reliable in a tight corner.

'Isn't it very demanding physically?' he went on now. 'Especially in the heat.'

'I'm lucky in that respect. It seems my body can put up with quite a lot. I go running in the hospital grounds early morning.'

'Last question, I promise. Are you afraid of danger?'

She looked at him very directly. 'Isn't everyone? On the other hand I'm single, no kids, only my mother to care about. And there's a war on. I don't think I'd panic, but nobody can know till it happens. What's all this about?'

He pushed his chair back, proffering a hand which she rose to take. 'It's an emergency. We need help. Someone said you might be the person to give it.'

'And what do you reckon?' she said.

'Thank you for indulging me, Sara. We'll be in touch.' He turned back. 'Oh by the way – have you ever been in the desert?'

'Not really.'

He smiled and walked away.

Now came another surprise because Henderson reappeared, though the Hungarian dancer hovered possessively in the background. The sight of Sara's mystery interviewer seemed to have got under Henderson's skin, and he was more loutish than ever.

'What did *he* want?' He nodded at Paddy's disappearing back.

'Just a chat amongst friends.'

'Oh yes! You want to be careful, a man like that.'

'I should've been more careful about *you*. Who is he, then? Do you actually know?'

Henderson shook his head. 'You don't *want* to know. Just watch out for yourself, before you get into bad company.'

'Goodnight Bill. Go back to your dancing girl.'

He did just that; no interest in her next move, how she was going to get 'home' — normally the minimum requirement for any man taking a girl out. She never saw him again. A few weeks later she heard he'd been barred from the Continental for having sex in the toilets with an American girl.

The morning after her mystery conversation at the hotel Sarah was summoned by Helmieh's Matron. She wasn't concerned, knowing the woman thought her competent, but she *was* curious. She sat in Matron's office and at once sensed that it was something serious.

'What I have to tell you is confidential,' Matron said. 'You mustn't repeat it to anyone. Have you heard of an outfit called the SAS?'

'No Matron.'

'Hm. It's new. Very hush hush. I believe you were talking to one of its members last night. They want to borrow you for a few weeks. They've heard about you somehow – that you get the job done. It's a feather in your cap.'

'Oh!'

'I'm extremely reluctant to let you go – you know how we're fixed here – but what they do is important, so I wouldn't stand in your way. That is, if you're sure you want to do it.'

'Yes but...'

'You want to know what 'it' is?'

'Yes, Matron.'

'That's where it gets difficult. They don't tell you much. They can't. As I understand it, they send small groups of men into the desert in Land-rovers and get up to no good. They don't have a doctor with them but they take a sort of medical orderly. That's where you would come in. Basic first aid. Their usual person is sick or something – anyway, not available. So they're looking for a replacement. But listen to me, Sara, this is no picnic. These men get hurt, and it can happen to you.'

'I'll do it,' Sara said.

Matron looked up sharply. 'Now hold on – you don't rush into a thing like this. Think about it first. It's as I'm telling you – the work will be dangerous.'

'I'd like to do it, Matron.'

This drew an undecipherable look, before Matron said 'So be it. I'll let them know you're available. And remember, not a word.'

'No Matron.'

*** *** ***

The corollary to Sara's little chat with Matron wasn't long delayed. A telephone call to the hospital asked if she could be free the following day to help plan supplies for the expedition. Then the man called Paddy – whom she'd met at the Cosmopolitan – arrived in a Jeep, bringing a companion he introduced as 'David Stirling'.

'He's kind've in charge,' Paddy intimated.

To Sara's eyes the Stirling person looked absurdly young to be in charge of anything. He told her they'd be driving across Cairo to collect her desert clothing from the unit's quartermaster, then on to a hospital to discuss medicines.

Sara was in the back of the open vehicle, the two men at the front with Stirling at the wheel. Before they'd gone a hundred yards she became seriously alarmed. Travelling on Cairo's roads was an unnerving experience at the best of times. The unwritten rule – if any rule existed – was that size took priority. Motorists habitually gave way to the juggernauts – lorries, trucks, the decrepit, backfiring local buses – with dire consequences if they failed to do so. In amongst them an army of old cars, taxis, gharries, donkey-drawn carts, scooters and bicycles vied for advantage, along with other outfits that defied description. (Sara saw a pure-bred filly drawing an open cart, its only cargo a heap of animal bones, with a swarm of flies in pursuit.) Ambling through the chaos was the occasional goat, whilst robed men and women, singly or in groups, made little scuttling movements between the onrushing vehicles. A regular hazard were man-holes from which the metal covers had been removed.

Over time this scene had become meat and drink to Sara, but the new ingredient was the manic driving of the David Stirling character. He weaved through the traffic at a speed Sara felt simply must lead to disaster, hurling imprecations at humans and livestock alike, standing on the brakes and generally behaving like a complete lunatic. The open structure of the Jeep meant there was nothing to prevent its occupants from being thrown overboard in the event of a collision. For the first time since arriving in Egypt Sara found herself shaking with fear. Paddy turned once in the front passenger seat to give a compliant little shrug, but seemed otherwise unconcerned.

After ten minutes of this Sara made up her mind. She shouted at Stirling, who heard nothing in the general cacophony, then leant over to pummel on his shoulders with her clenched fists. Clearly surprised, the man turned in the driving seat – *not* her desired outcome at all – and eventually acceded to her shriek of 'STOP', manoeuvring his vehicle to the roadside where it halted beside a moth-eaten camel.

'What's the problem?' he enquired, barely audible against the muezzin that had struck up from an adjacent mosque.

Hoping that the shaking of her hands weren't too obvious, Sara did her best to sound calm and composed. 'Mr Stirling, sooner or later you are going to kill someone driving in this ridiculous manner, and I'm not prepared for it to be me.'

'I've not had any complaints before,' he said mildly.

Paddy made a throat-clearing sound. 'You do step on it a bit, David.'

'Why don't you write down the address we're making for,' Sara persisted. 'I shall obtain a gharry and meet you there.'

He swivelled right round to scrutinise her more closely. 'No, that won't be necessary. I'll tone it down a bit.'

'I'd appreciate that.'

For the rest of the journey he drove more conventionally and Sara's pulse rate returned to normal. They drew up before a military building and got out. Paddy gave Sara a wink.

'That was a first,' he murmured.

Inside, relations with Stirling remained somewhat constrained, and it was Paddy who gave her the run-down on clothing.

'I believe you've no experience of the desert,' he said.

'Just two days on the fringes.' She described the fledgling

hospital near Suez.

'Well you won't believe it,' he went on, 'But the desert's a really cold place first thing. Wear the warmest part of your nurse's clothing above the waist, and I'll find you a greatcoat and a blanket.'

'Blimey.'

'I'm not kidding. But by mid-day, with the sun up, you'll need to wear very little. I expect you've got shorts, and...' He reached into one of the cupboards. 'Here's an Arab head-dress. Anywhere near the ocean there's a breeze, and this thing flaps about, keeps you cool. Now as for footwear, in those sandy conditions we use leather sandals. Sit down here and try some on for size.'

Once she'd been sorted out they drove on (more cautiously this time) to a hospital – specifically to a room full of drugs and equipment. Paddy handed her a list.

'This documents all the stuff your predecessor took on his last mission. We thought you might go for the same again.'

She turned to him and to Stirling. 'Can I go back to basics? How long will we be away? What are the risks and when will we face them? And what kind of risks?'

This time it was Stirling who answered. 'You know, Miss Cox...'

'Sara.'

'Sara. For most of a trip like this the risks are low, unless we're unlucky. The men's health would be be 100% if only it weren't for those wretched desert sores. I expect you've heard about them – caused by friction from the sand. They drive us all to distraction.'

'Yes, of course. It's possible I can help with that.'

'You think so! It is a long-standing problem, Miss...um, Sara.'

'The thing is, we've got a captured German doctor in Helmieh.'

'A Kraut! Is that wise?'

'We keep an eye on the man. He's not in very good shape actually. But you know what science people are like – always willing to share information. It seems the Germans have tracked down a particular bacterium in desert sores. They treat it with dressings made of Vaseline and sulphonamide. If the problem with your people is as bad as you say, I'd like to make up some dressings before we leave. Then the men can carry their own dressings with them.'

Stirling looked surprised, almost pleased, by her suggestion. Both men lurked in the background while Sara gave the hospital staff more requests: dressings, plaster of Paris, splints, larger amounts of codeine and morphia than were given on the original list, and something for dysentery, which was never far away in Egypt.

She had one other matter to raise. 'I'd like to add something that isn't on the list,' she told the two SAS men, 'And that's plasma. Only I don't know if it's available here. It's a new item, just coming on stream.'

'What is plasma exactly?' Paddy asked.

'It's a component of blood. A very important component.'

Stirling was looking sceptical. 'Do you think it's really necessary?'

'Plasma is very good for treating shock in casualties. We should take some if it's available.'

'Then let's ask,' said Paddy.

They found the hospital had a supply, stored in litre bottles. Sara was told she could have two cartons of them. She thanked the staff and turned to Stirling.

'Then that's it. We have what we need.'

He stepped forward. 'Sara, I like the way you've gone about this. You clearly know what you're doing, and that's always appreciated in this unit. Thank you.'

She knew this was the closest she'd get to an apology for the earlier incident, and it was more than good enough.

'Thank *you*,' she replied.

~ Four ~

With the SAS in the Libyan desert, November 1941

Within the week Sara had temporarily wound up her duties at
Helmieh. She was driven to an afternoon rendezvous at the
SAS's Cairo HQ to meet the men earmarked for the new
operation. She felt on edge but also excited about the
experiences ahead. Matron's warning about danger barely
entered her head. The meeting took place in a room containing
tables with food and moderate amounts of drink. She sensed
immediately the men's curiosity at having a female participant
in what was normally an all-male world. There was a lot of
joking and fooling about but nothing that made her remotely
uncomfortable.

The next morning they were under way by 7am; eighteen
men distributed amongst five Chevrolet Jeeps and a lorry. Sara
had a good spot in a Jeep with just the driver in front and Paddy
beside her in the back, since he'd apparently decided to take
her under his wing. They'd gone by the Delta road to
Alexandria. Immediately, Sara felt glad she'd accepted the job,
surrounded as she was by the sprawling excess of cultivation,
with camels everywhere she looked. It occurred to her how
little she'd seen of the country, marooned at Helmieh with the
hospital and the tawdry nite-spots and little else besides. As
the sun rose, the breeze made travelling in an open vehicle very
pleasant. The downside came when the party stopped for lunch

and swarms of mosquitoes descended, whilst in the watery verges of the roadside hundreds of frogs made their presence felt.

Her spirits leapt again when the Jeep lurched onto a broad tarmac road and the Mediterranean came into sight. She gave an involuntary cry of delight.

Paddy too laughed in exhilaration. 'Always gets people first time. Make the most of it Sara. We shan't be on the tarmac for long.'

'How far does it go?' she asked.

'About a thousand miles along the North Africa coast, to Tripoli and beyond.'

'Gracious!'

They were travelling steadily, with the great, liberating stretch of water to their right. Suddenly Sara wanted his opinion on some matters that had puzzled her for months. She turned towards him on the leather seating.

'Paddy, us nurses in Helmieh are always banging on about the war, but there's stuff I've never got straight in my head. Will you advise me?'

"I'll have a go.'

'OK then. A thousand miles along the coast, you say. So where does Libya start?'

'About half way along. And out there to the south...' He

pointed left, away from the ocean, 'It's all desert – give or take the occasional oasis. Just sand and sand and more sand for thousands of square miles. It's an area not that much smaller than India.'

'How horrible!'

He grinned. He was always grinning. 'You think so?'

'I wouldn't want to be stuck out there.'

'Hm. There are people who like the desert, you know. Some people even love it. Reserve judgement, maybe? There'll be plenty of time to make up your mind.'

She sat thoughtfully while the Jeep convoy negotiated a dodgy stretch of tarmac, then came back with more questions.

'So look, when Mussolini took over all this desert...that's exactly what I don't get. I mean, honestly, is all this sand worth fighting for?'

He shifted his big frame. 'Don't forget the Huns have joined in now. That makes a big difference. And nearly all the actual fighting takes place within sixty miles of this road.'

'So then – is all this sand worth having?' she almost shouted at him.

He spread both arms expansively. 'No. It's ridiculous.'

'*What*!' Baffled, she reached out to punch his arm.

'Striking an officer,' he said. 'Forty lashes. Look, some people talk about us protecting a route to the oil fields in the Persian Gulf. Oil is important, of course. But if you think about it, this is the only place in the world where we're actually fighting Germans. Mostly the war's been about them swanning into countries and taking over. So for this reason the Middle East war has sort've caught the public's imagination. There's no backing out now. Though if you insist, I can leave you at the side of the road.'

She laughed. 'I'll stick around for the time being.'

Sara was not to know it, but progress on the road was sublimely simple compared to everything that came afterwards. All too soon their little convoy plunged off the tarmac and onto the sandy desert that would be their travel surface for the next few days. Their pace slowed and vehicles jolted on the rough ground. She was surprised to feel weariness creeping into her body, after a day she considered less taxing than one spent at Helmieh, and was glad when Stirling halted the convoy to say they were stopping there for the night. Soon after that the darkness came down with surprising abruptness. The man who'd been designated as the party's cook set to work and before long they were all sitting round eating a kind of stew with tinned potatoes. Following which she learnt that the plates and utensils could be cleaned through the medium of sand just as efficiently as with soap and water. And even more surprisingly, that officers and men shared the menial tasks between them. She remarked upon it to Paddy.

He nodded. 'You can see why, can't you. Out in the desert we're all dependent on each other. Everyone does everything.

No place for the usual egos. David Stirling always takes the first sentry duty, to make the point.'

'I'm impressed,' she said.

'Actually,' he went on, 'The most important people in the group are the specialists, because they can't be replaced.'

She'd noticed something of this during the day. The group's mechanic had already been in action sorting an engine problem. Another man in the party spoke fluent Italian. Another was the navigator, described by Paddy as the one they could least afford to lose. He was universally known as 'Theo', and when Sara asked him why she found he came from the same area of Finsbury Park as her mother. As most of the men finished their duties for the day he was still at work. He called her across to explain what he was doing.

'We have a compass mounted on one of the leading Jeeps,' he said. 'But of course that can never be a hundred per cent accurate. That's where this little item comes in.'

'And what is that?'

'It's called a theodolite.'

She laughed. 'Theo – of course.'

'They're very hard to get hold of. You use them to plot your position by the stars.'

'It looks pretty complicated to me,' she said. 'You ought to get paid extra.'

'Actually, I do. Anyone who passes the navigator tests gets paid an extra shilling a day.'

'A whole shilling! Wow!'

With the meal over there was little else for the men to do. A couple of them were reading by the light of Hurricane lamps, but most talked quietly in small groups or prepared for shut-eye. Sara took her sleeping bag from the Jeep and lay on it trying to absorb a scene that had no parallel in her previous life. The murmurings of the men were the only sounds in a profound silence.

Paddy came across to check on her. As with all the SAS party he was tentative about encroaching on her space, sitting himself down a few feet away. 'Everything OK?' he asked. 'How do you feel about the desert now?'

She gave a rueful smile. 'I may have been a bit hasty in forming a judgement.'

He grinned but said nothing.

'Do you know Paddy, I suddenly realised – there are no mosquitoes here.'

'No. And no flies.'

'And no flies. How marvellous. And...' She gestured around with a sweep of the hand. 'This sky. This *enormous* purple sky. Golly.'

'And you've not even mentioned...'

74

She laughed softly. 'The stars, yes. Hundreds, thousands of stars.'

Some of the men looked in their direction and she was suddenly aware of her voice, and its tone striking a new note in their company.

'And here I am amongst it all,' she told Paddy. 'One woman with all you blokes.'

'It's all right Sara, they like having you here. I've noticed a subtle change of atmosphere already. There's never been a woman before. It's all good.'

'Sorry, I wasn't fishing for compliments.'

'And I wasn't giving one. Just telling you how it is.' He rose to his feet. 'Goodnight Sara. Make sure you're in that sleeping bag before you drop off. It gets very cold at night.'

She did as he said and remembered little more except waking into absolute silence, for a moment confused not to be in her Helmieh tent. From the faintness of stars in the sky she judged it to be about an hour before dawn. They'd told her this could be the time for 'ablutions' (the euphemism always used), and she forced herself to creep from the warm sleeping bag. Ablutions presented a challenge for a woman amongst men. She knew the SAS rule about never moving beyond sight of her companions, but certain things were best kept private. She ventured as far off as she dared, noting some shadowy movements on the periphery, and was back in camp just as most of the men were rising.

She sat with cook and a few others drinking a cup of hot, sweet tea, and had her water bottle filled from a supply held in the lorry. Paddy had impressed upon her the unwritten SAS code about drinking water: one bottle per person per day; no drinking before mid-day; use it in small sips; never lend your water to anyone else.

The first two hours of travelling, before the sun disclosed its full heat, were the best for everyone. At no stage did Sara know what distance they were from their objective. Stirling had told them before starting that the target would be known by as few people as possible. 'Otherwise, with the best will in the world,' he observed dryly, 'We may arrive and find a welcoming party in place.' This constraint freed her mind of everything except their snail-like progress across the landscape. Not knowing the terrain, she was astonished when the uniform flatness gave way to something resembling – against all expectations – a mountain range; the ugliest formations imaginable, scraped up from nowhere, forming a barrier that could be skirted but never crossed.

'The Qattara Depression,' Paddy muttered, as if that explained everything. 'Ugly bugger, isn't it.' He said they'd soon be crossing from Egypt into Libya. Apparently the Italians had as yet made no effort to close the non-existent border.

In mid-afternoon, with the sun at its hottest, they were held up for a couple of hours. Sara, new to scrutinising the desert's surface, found it tricky to distinguish between easy and hard going for the vehicles. Now and then one of the Jeeps had become stuck in the soft sand, but by dint of careful manoeuvring – backwards, she noted, and always gently by degrees, sometimes with the help of sand trays placed under the wheels – the drivers had managed to extricate themselves. Unfortunately it was now the lorry's turn, as it became hopelessly mired in deep sand. There were long faces amongst the men who stood round the stricken vehicle.

'Everyone's looking very fed up,' Sara remarked to Chris, the cook. 'Does it mean we'll have to abandon the lorry?'

'Lord no, Sara, that'll never happen. We wouldn't be left with any drinking water, for a start. No, they're miffed because we'll have to unload the lorry before it can be freed, and in the hottest part of the day. Don't worry, it's a regular occurrence with lorries – the bastards.' He kicked out furiously at one of the vehicle's innocent tyres.

It *was* extremely hot, and the last thing Sara felt like was lifting heavy supplies, but she was also determined not to be the one who stood and watched. She pitched in with the others, starting with her precious medical items. Paddy was at once across saying 'You don't have to do this, Sara,' and she responded with 'I absolutely do,' and reckoned from the men's sideways glances and murmured comments that she might have taken a small step towards acceptance by the SAS brotherhood.

For an hour and a half the men worked with a methodical, cussed persistence, and again she noted that Paddy and Stirling were prominent amongst them. The sun's blazing orb came down with undreamed of ferocity, inspiring an emotion akin to hatred. The men retained their head coverings but were stripped to the waist, and halfway through Sara muttered 'Damn it' and stripped off her blouse to reveal just a bra beneath. Afterwards Stirling commented that the unit's efforts had redoubled at that moment.

A ragged cheer went up as the final piece of equipment was removed and they began the business of jolting the vehicle free, again with a gentleness that seemed inappropriate to the lorry's obstreperous bulk. Men thrust forward wherever they could find purchase on the great, inanimate beast, till it finally lumbered clear. Then came the task of putting all its contents back in place again. Afterwards Stirling announced an additional drink of water and the troops sprawled about sipping it in the lorry's shadow.

Sara couldn't rest straight away because one man had cut his hand quite badly. She administered stitches, an antiseptic and a dressing, watched by a ghoulish bunch of the unfortunate fellow's comrades. Stirling walked past bestowing a terse 'Well done'.

Sara's body ached that night as she lay awake in the sleeping bag, and for some reason she began thinking about her mother. This was unusual and she struggled to explain it. She longed to receive some word from home but there was no form of effective communication between them. This hadn't stopped her from writing a few times but she knew her letters would carry no meaning. The distance between mother and daughter seemed unfathomable. A tear ran down her face and she brushed it impatiently away. She hardly ever cried.

Over the next couple of days the rhythm of desert travelling did not noticeably vary from what she'd experienced already. She took care to enjoy its pleasures and began adjusting to the vicissitudes. Since one day's experience was much like another, any variation stood out. So one morning they passed the remains of a camel that had died many years before; fascinated, she peered inside the dried-up skin to see the beast's shrivelled organs. Then on the second night a yellow scorpion approached her sleeping bag and was quickly despatched.

For the most part the men seemed content in their desert setting, and Sara was unaware of any quarrels or difficult moments. She was impressed. It would have been understandable if they were on edge, given the imminent affray with the enemy, when some of their number were likely to be injured or killed.

When on the move they liked to sing, and she was only mildly embarrassed when a fervent rendering of 'If you were the only girl in the world' sprang up across all six vehicles, with the singers gesticulating in her direction.

The big fear of every soldier in the desert was an enemy plane flying overhead, with its likely corollary of deadly machine gun fire against the vehicles below. The pre-planned response to this eventuality was vehicles scattering in all directions and meeting up later at a rendezvous, but it meant at least one Jeep having a very bad time. Fortunately the skies had remained clear.

More by accident than design, the hour before the evening

meal had become a sort of surgery, when Sara attended to minor health concerns amongst the men. Once or twice she suspected they'd looked for problems in order to enjoy female attention, but there were plenty of genuine public health problems, not to mention the ever-present desert sores. As usual she never had reason to feel awkwardness about the way she was treated. Joking and daft fooling about was normal behaviour for the SAS, but there was none of the suggestive language or unnecessary touching she experienced on evenings out with British officers.

Without doubt the best moments of her days came in the time before sleep, when the temperature had cooled and she lay watching the stars in the sky. One evening when the radio operator was toying with his machine (which often refused to co-operate) he chanced upon a German broadcasting station, and the desert was invaded by the strains of Marlene Dietrich singing 'Lili Marlene', a song popular with Allied and Axis troops alike. The sound of German lyrics echoing across the empty sands made a curious impression upon her.

Sara had lost all sense of direction during their travels around the desert, but when she talked to the men they came up with various theories. The consensus was that they'd forged west some way into the Libyan desert, before striking out north towards the Mediterranean and the coastal road. Though nobody said it out loud she understood that the target would be an Italian airfield.

Stirling offered a confirmation of this when he called the men together early one morning. The idea was that they'd leave the lorry at a rendezvous three kilometres from an airfield, in a spot that offered natural camouflage properties. Then in the small hours all the SAS Jeeps would quietly approach the target. It seemed that he and Paddy had considered two different plans. The conventional one would be to drive in with machine guns blazing, some Jeeps holding the centre ground to counter Italian fire, others circling the airfield to blast the Italians' planes with guns and grenades.

After consideration they were taking a different option, because the Italians were famously lax at posting sentries. With luck they'd have left the airfield unguarded or they may have posted a sentry who'd then fallen asleep. The SAS would hold several Jeeps on the perimeter, ready to go in with guns firing if needed, but initially men would enter on foot, scouting the area to drop Lewes bombs into the cockpits of Italian fighter planes. If they were lucky this would minimize casualties on the SAS side. He concluded 'But as we know, plans fall apart the moment they come into contact with the enemy, so stay alert and be ready for anything.'

As soon as he'd finished speaking the men gathered in groups to chatter about the assignment, and Stirling sensibly allowed them time to do so. Sara had one burning question and she buttonholed Theo the navigator about it. 'Well miss, Jock Lewes was a very clever chap,'
Theo responded. He reckoned he could save lives if there was a bomb that exploded a while *after* it had been put in place. I can't tell you how exactly but think of an acid that burns away a thin wire. This releases a spring, which leads to an explosion

and a fire. With any luck the bloke who places the bomb has got well clear by the time it goes off. Well miss, we've got dozens of those explosive little buggers with us, all ready and waiting for the Iti planes.'

He was interrupted by Stirling, who said he wanted 'a word' with Sara. The two of them went to sit in one of the Jeeps. 'What I didn't say just then,' he told her,' Was where *you* will be in this plan.'

'And of course I wondered,' she said.

'We'll have one man staying with the lorry back at the rendezvous, and that will be your position too. Any casualties will be rushed back to you in the Jeeps.'

She stared at him. 'I thought you said the lorry would be three kilometres from the airfield.'

'That's right, Sara.'

'Then no,' was her response. 'If there are casualties the first few minutes are likely be crucial in handling them successfully. My being at the rendezvous won't be good enough.'

'Well that's where your predecessor was the last time we did this, and that's where you'll be. I'm responsible for your safety, Sara, and I don't want you anywhere near the fighting. Forgive me but this isn't about you proving how courageous you are.'

He started to move away but she grabbed his arm. 'I'm sorry sir, but you've got this wrong.' The 'sir', which she rarely used with him, was an indication of her seriousness. 'I'm *not* a brave person – that's not it at all – but I agreed to leave my usual work to come on this madcap venture, amongst a group of raving maniacs by the way, and I don't want to feel afterwards that I've wasted my time. If there's any point in my being here I need to be near the action. Sir.'

Sara had surprised herself speaking out in this fashion, but it was part of a long voyage of self-discovery. A year earlier she wouldn't have said boo to a goose. These days she seemed ready to flex her muscles and express an opinion. She sat in the Jeep waiting uneasily for his reaction.

Stirling left a long pause. 'All right then,' he said eventually, 'Against my better judgement you'll be in position just outside the airfield.' He clambered from the Jeep, then turned back to her. 'And you are quite wrong, Sara – you certainly *are* a courageous person. Believe me, that's something I do know about.'

Fewer than 12 hours later Sara found herself sitting in a Jeep just outside an Italian airfield, at 2am in the small hours. The moon shone brightly – probably brighter than Stirling would have wished – but her view of the airfield was blocked by a line of foliage. What she could see was several SAS Jeeps about a hundred yards ahead, with manned machine guns mounted fore and aft and a driver at the wheel of each. The soft muttering of their idling engines just about reached her. Two more unmanned Jeeps were at her back, positioned for a quick escape if this proved necessary.

Alone in her Jeep, Sara could just about hear the

Mediterranean breaking upon the shore beyond. At this moment she could imagine the SAS men prowling about the airfield with their home-made Lewes bombs. She was tremendously aware of her own heart thumping in her chest. Did that mean she was afraid? Or was she really courageous, as Stirling had suggested. Her main feelings were admiration for the men now out in the airfield; men she'd sat with that morning as they drank their early cups of tea, who had obeyed without question the order to attack and might at any moment get a bullet in the gut for their pains. They demonstrated a courage that was beyond her experience or understanding.

These reflections came to an end as the silence was shattered by a single violent explosion. Then came the sound of several machine guns firing. The Jeeps ahead of her revved their engines and streamed forward. Very soon there were different types of explosion, one after another in a steady succession, and a series of red streaks decorated the night sky.

She tried to remain calm and ready for any action required. After some minutes the three Jeeps returned from the fray one after the other. This time they were bursting with SAS men who, in the confusion, were shouting over each other, leaving their intentions unclear.

In the first Jeep a body lay still across the back seat. Sara ran across to him shining her torch, which revealed a bullet wound in the forehead. There was no pulse and she told his companions the man was dead.

The second Jeep bore a man who was very much alive, and

bleeding heavily to prove it. She got his mates to carry him to her original vehicle, which contained the medical supplies.

'It's my leg,' the victim said, trying not to look panicky, and leaving blood all over the seat. All around her vehicles were noisily manoeuvring. She examined the wound by torchlight.

'OK,' she said, 'It's Stephen, isn't it. You've taken a bullet in the thigh.'

'What do you think miss?' The usual anxious question from a wounded soldier.

She got him to twist on the seat so as to free up the back of his thigh, cleaned away the blood then used the torch again. 'Good news,' she said, and saw his expression lift. 'The bullet's come out the other side. And also good news that it didn't hit you a bit higher up,' she added, and this time was rewarded with a grin. The bleeding was relentless and she told him she'd need to put heavy pressure on it. She did so, even using her knee at one point. There were anxious noises coming from men in a third Jeep and she shouted that she'd be with them as soon as possible. She cleaned Stephen's wound, applied the antiseptic sulphonamide and plugged both holes. After a gauze dressing she made him keep still for a transfusion of the invaluable plasma, thanking her lucky stars that some had been available. Stephen was calmer now and regarded her face steadily as the plasma entered his blood stream.

'Will you marry me?' he said eventually.

She laughed. 'I'll make a note of your request. Meanwhile, please keep still.'

All the time she'd been attending to Stephen's wound Sara was conscious of that agitation emanating from men in the third vehicle. As she stood washing her hands and cleaning blood from her clothing, one of the men approached her.

'It's Theo,' he said, and the stress in his voice was unmistakeable.

A complication presented itself in the form of David Stirling, his gaze fixed on the airfield. The noise of battle had evaporated though the sky remained red from burning planes.

'I'm really sorry, Sara,' he told her, 'But we have to get away from here. Sooner or later the Iti's will come looking for us. I know you have things to do, but can you work on the move?'

'I'll do what I can,' she said. 'Give me a moment.'

She went to collect her medical gear and found that someone had cleaned up. Most of the blood had gone from the Jeep's back seat. She knew it was Paddy; though unwounded, he had stains all over his clothing.

The men distributed themselves amongst the six vehicles and engines revved ready for the move out. The speed of thought and action from these people, whom she'd usually seen when they were fooling about, impressed her greatly. These were professional soldiers being professional when it mattered. She jumped into the back of the Jeep where Theo lay injured and the driver stepped on the accelerator. The unit moved out in orderly formation, sustaining a steady pace across the rough ground. Fortunately Stirling was not one of the drivers. No sign of pursuit came from the Italians.

She eased into place beside the wounded man. The Jeeps were on dimmed headlights and she used a torch. She kept her features free from emotion, which called for an effort. The fact that she knew the victim made things worse. He was just about conscious, slumped white-faced on the uncomfortable seating. His left arm below the elbow was a horrible mess. She wondered what could possibly have caused it: a grenade perhaps, or a landmine, but on the arm...? She touched his shoulder gently. 'I'm here to patch you up, Theo. How did this happen, do you remember?'

He shook his head. Said he 'wasn't sure', and didn't much seem to care. 'Do what you can,' was all he would say.

'Of course I will.' She could see the driver's troubled expression in his mirror, a blend of concern with that ever-present thought process — 'Thank god it didn't happen to me'. The bare landscape skimmed past as they bowled along at 30 miles an hour.

'I'll try not to move your arm,' she told Theo, 'But I must have a good look.'

What her torch revealed was not something she wanted to dwell upon. Nurses were trained to accept realities but there were limits. The stew of tortured flesh and bone didn't resemble a forearm at all. She searched in her bag for a morphia capsule, then changed her mind and decided to inject, unsure whether the man could swallow properly. She found her indelible pencil and wrote the time of the injection on his forehead.

As soon as the relief showed on Theo's face she took a closer look at his arm. Mixed up with the flesh were various fragments of matter and various impurities. To clean the wound as it stood would be a form of torture. She decided then and there that her job was to keep the man alive; to get him quickly to a hospital and the attentions of a proper surgeon. She gave him sulphonamide and a dose of plasma, and put a light dressing on the arm. He was asleep or unconscious, either way a blessing. She packed two blankets around him to counter shock and thought as she did so that it was like putting an Elastoplast on a gaping wound.

When they reached the rendezvous Paddy materialised by her side. At her behest he lifted Theo's body and carried it to a mattress in the back of the lorry. Sara intended to follow but it didn't happen. When she woke it was to find *herself* in Paddy's arms, carried as if she weighed nothing at all.

'Put me down, Paddy,' she told him. 'I can walk, you know.'

'Just like any other robot,' he said. 'Pipe down and go to sleep.'

She woke nine hours later to find the lorry in motion and herself curled on the seat beside the driver. She cursed and scrambled to the back of the vehicle, where Theo was dozing fitfully. The man with him – whose name was George – gave a little shake of the head.

'Am I glad to see you, miss.'

She took Theo's pulse and gave another morphine injection. A bit later on he regained consciousness. He wasn't in great pain and seemed fairly clear-headed.

'So what's to become of me?' he asked.

'You'll be delivered into the hands of a first-rate surgeon in Cairo. He'll sort you out.'

'You think so, do you.' The worst patients were the ones with a clear-eyed view of their condition.

She knew - and thought he knew – that speed was important with an injury of this kind. But as luck would have it the plan to get Theo back rapidly didn't work out. Following the SAS attack, the Italians sent up a plane to look for the offenders. The first Sara knew of it was hearing a fighter plane roar overhead and feeling the lorry accelerate across uneven ground. 'Now we're for it,' observed George, but curiously – as they were later to discover – the pilot chose to attack one of the Jeeps rather than the sitting target of the lorry. By a pre-arranged plan the SAS vehicles scrambled and met up again at a nominated place. And of course when they did meet, one of the Jeeps was missing. The others went out to search, but the grim endgame was all but inevitable. When they reconvened hours later the story was soon told. The unlucky Jeep had been machine-gunned and set on fire. The driver was killed, a second man thrown from the vehicle with a broken leg and a third escaped without a scratch. So Sara had another patient, and whole company stood round as they buried the dead man in the desert. They left a small cross to mark a forsaken spot that would rarely be witnessed again.

The episode meant a further delay in getting Theo to hospital. Setting off again, Stirling kept his people moving as quickly as possible, but desert travel did not lend itself to short-cuts. Sara was all too aware of the risks attached to an injury like Theo's, having witnessed them often enough in Helmieh. On the plus side the injured limb became numb, because loss of blood had led to the skin tissue dying. But on the third morning Theo's arm began to turn black and give off an unpleasant smell, which she'd feared from the outset because it indicated gangrene. Worse still, she recognised a virulent form of the condition known as gas gangrene. She knew full well what these developments implied and it seemed Theo knew as well. He'd remained conscious and surprisingly calm. He didn't once used the fearsome 'g' word, but she knew that he understood. He raised the subject when George was also in the lorry.

'You've been amazing, Sara,' he told her, 'But I wonder if you'd now go one better.'

'What *do* you mean?' she said, fearful that she knew already.

'I know how much they value your work at the hospital,' he said. 'You must have attended plenty of amputations there.'

'Oh Theo! You overrate my abilities. And you know there's always a high degree of risk, even in the antiseptic conditions of a hospital. In the back of a lorry, with sand all over the place...'

'But would you be allowed to attempt it?'

'I don't understand...'

'I mean, is there any danger of you getting into trouble. If so, then it's out of the question. I want that to be clear.'

That was the moment she made up her mind. His generosity of spirit had sparked her own best instincts.

'You'd better talk to Paddy?' she said. 'Tell him what you want.'

'Of course.'

She got Paddy to see him while she and George went outside. George approached her as she stood staring moodily at the horizon.

'Can I have a word, miss?'

'Of course you can.'

'The thing is, a lot of blokes find operations and that hard to watch. People even pass out sometimes.'

She looked at him curiously. 'I'm not sure what you're saying.'

'It's just that I don't have that problem. I'm not bothered by them physical things. My missus, she says I ought to see a psychiatrist. What I mean is, if you need someone to help, miss, I'd like to do it. I dunno, maybe you'll need some extra force, or something like that.'

She could have kissed him. 'If you're really sure about this, it would help very much. Extra force, hm...I'd do it at the elbow, so there'd be no need to cut through bone...' As she spoke the operation suddenly unfolded in her imagination, and she took George by the arm. 'Come on, let's get ready straight away. Every minute that passes lowers his chances.'

It was dark in the body of the lorry and Paddy arranged for some Hurricane lamps to be set up; he often knew what she needed before she knew herself. Stirling called by to say encouraging words. It seemed to her that half the unit was getting involved. Cook arranged for the utensils she would use to be sterilised in boiling water.

She started with some anaesthetic capsules and hoped that Theo would pass out, which he did without uttering a word. George hovered beside her in the flickering light of the lamps. She could hear the men moving about outside, preparing for the day's travelling.

It troubled her that she knew only what her memory had retained, for there was no chance of consulting medical reference books. But once she began, her years of training and experience kicked in and the doubts receded. She cleaned the whole area of skin with a saline solution (cook again). She knew that the skin tissue must be healthy on the amputation site and that she should cut below the level of the bone, so flaps of skin could be stitched to form a smooth, rounded stump. There was limited bleeding as she cut away the dead tissue, but in any case George was on hand to clean and mop up. True to his word, he was not squeamish about sights that other men might have found repellent, and was methodical in all his movements. She

92

made sure the nerves were severed well above the stump to reduce the risk of pressure pain, and closed off the blood vessels. It all seemed to take longer than she remembered, and half way through the stitching up process she was sweating profusely. As she laid aside the needle to mop her face George picked it up and completed the job, at least as neatly as she'd managed herself. She used Pentothal and the last resources of plasma. She finished as the sun's rays were stoking up the temperature in the lorry, and suddenly feeling faint, half toppled over. George intercepted her fall and pressed a flask of drinking water into her hands.

'Well done, miss,' he told her.

'You were a tremendous help.'

She climbed over the tailgate and jumped down. As her feet hit the ground she staggered, and again would have gone over had Paddy not been there to prevent it. She wondered how he did that – being available whenever help was needed. She gave him a progress report, stressing George's contribution.

'I know you need to get moving,' she said. 'Don't worry, George and I will watch over him.'

Of course Theo's survival would depend as much upon his own resilience as on anything she might do. She knew that. All the same she and George stayed in the lorry for the next 24 hours. They helped him make small alterations to his position. They offered water when he was conscious. When his breathing grew weak they prepared to give artificial respiration, but he always rallied. Every half hour they cleaned the dust off his recumbent form.

In the small hours they were still there, now down to one Hurricane lamp. The only sounds came from men sleeping on the sand outside – snoring, sometimes of a gargantuan nature, occasionally a rampant breaking of wind.

Around 3am Sara sat up abruptly, snorting herself awake, and for the umpteenth time put a hand on Theo's forehead. George was propped up against the tailboard, his face a horrible puffy sight, red eyes open. He never seemed to sleep.

He nodded towards Theo. 'What do you think, miss?'

'I wish I knew. These first 24 hours are so important.'

'Nobody could've done more.'

Without any warning Theo, who had barely spoken during the day, began to sing in a surprisingly firm voice. Sara's head went up. She'd heard this happen once or twice with recovering patients in Helmieh, but never anything so coherent. There was no discernible melody. It was neither pleasant nor unpleasant. She looked across at George, who gave no sign of hearing anything at all. It was hard to imagine what such a sound might signify, coming from the subconscious of someone faltering on the brink of death. She knew better than to invest in hope, much as she wanted to. Nurses had an aversion to optimism that bordered on superstition.

When she woke next morning Theo was conscious and awake. George greeted her with a broad grin. Paddy's head poked over the tailgate. He'd brought breakfast for anyone who wanted it. He'd not heard Theo singing. Later she found that none of the men had; they seemed disinclined to believe in it.

Over the next three days, as the convoy made its painstaking way back to Cairo, Theo grew stronger and more articulate. Sara's other patients also held their own. A few hours out of the capital Stirling asked her to come into his Jeep. He said he'd talked to Paddy and they wanted her to consider a permanent attachment to the SAS. She told him the previous few weeks had been the most meaningful of her life but that she must return to work at Helmieh hospital.

Endings were often anti-climactic and this was no different. Sara felt dazed, as though she'd forgotten something very important. The entire unit came one by one to say goodbye as she stood shyly beside one of the Jeeps. She shook their hands and said 'thank you', with special words for Paddy and George. She had a final word with Theo, and wrote some notes on him for the military hospital. Then Paddy drove her back to Helmieh. They barely exchanged a word en route.

*** *** ***

Helmieh was in darkness when Paddy dropped her off. After the wide open spaces of the desert, everything about the place looked cramped. She decided to delay checking in till the

95

following morning and went straight to her tent. That too was dark, which meant Rose had a late duty. She lit the Hurricane lamp, reviving echoes of her work in the lorry.

On her pillow were a circular from the hospital and a welcome back note from Rose 'for whenever you get here'. And there was an envelope bearing UK stamps and a British postmark. This was so unusual that she barely gave it a glance; she was a stranger to the usual excitement about 'mail from home'. Even the handwriting on the envelope, like that of a small child, failed to pique her interest. She almost ignored the communication, feeling bone-weary, her head full of the desert, but finally picked the thing up and slit it open. She took out the single sheet of paper, gasped, and sat down on the bed to read.

Sara

I try to write to my girl becos I miss her a lot. Sorry for mistakes there will be some but is not bad is it for an ignorent woman. I think of you all the time. I hope you are safe. I know you will do a good job. Your letters I like a lot so pleas send more. Thank you for every thing. I wish you are here. Keep safe. Love, your mother.

The letter was short, but she knew its writing would have devoured hours of intense concentration, no doubt with a dictionary at hand. Of course the handwriting was unfamiliar because she hadn't seen it before. No-one had. As she read,

96

Sara was thinking back to their last meeting when she'd urged her mother to take English lessons from the teacher who lived round the corner. During all her time abroad she'd barely given this a thought. She realised now she'd assumed her mother wouldn't be able to handle the plan. Instead of which here was a confirmation of her mother's intelligence and industry, and more than that a generosity of spirit. And reading it now for the first time she thought of a hundred things she wanted to say in reply. She could hardly wait to put pen to paper.

She stayed there in the gloomy light, perched on the edge of the bed with her shoulders shaking, and reflected that she had never in her life felt so full of optimism.

~ Five ~

With Karim   1942

Following her time in Libya with the SAS, Sara settled back into the work at Helmieh easily enough. She missed the desert – which came as a big surprise to her – and in more honest moments she even missed her proximity to the fighting. But by necessity the SAS world began to fade into the shadows, eve+n though Paddy visited her one lunchtime with a card signed by every man who'd survived the attack on the Italian airfield. And best of all she had a visit from Theo; a smiling, fit Theo, apparently adjusted to life with one arm. There'd been no official repercussions arising from a mere nurse undertaking amputation, though in the hidebound world of medicine this was something she'd feared. She suspected Stirling had put in a word with the authorities. She also felt there might have been consequences had the result of the operation been different.

There was one way in which Sara's Helmieh life changed from what had gone before. Even before the SAS adventure she'd begun to tire of the recurrent dinner dates with British officers. To an extent they'd helped to knock the corners off a shy young girl with a limited experience of life, and she was grateful for that. She'd learnt that she was attractive to these men, who were happy enough to wine and dine her, but she also knew most of them were looking for more. Yet she herself hadn't come across a man she wanted to be close to, let alone in Gina's

98

sense of 'bagging a husband'. This also applied to the whole business of sex, with which she felt completely at sea. Was this, she wondered, to do with the attitudes of the men concerned. She never forgot Rose commenting 'The officer wards are always unpopular'. The only officers Sara had become close to were those in the SAS, but that was a different story.

She was rescued from becoming a total hermit by her Italian friend. Gina had discovered a hotel, complete with dance floor, that permitted two girls to visit together. When Sara could get away for a couple of days she would go into Cairo and stay at Gina's Garden City flat. More often than not they'd have an evening meal at Groppi's and then go on to this hotel, where they could dance with a variety of single men, most of whom seemed respectable.

So it was that Sara arrived at Gina's one Sunday afternoon in September. Following their usual custom the two girls sat out on the balcony drinking mint tea. Sounds of Cairo street life drifted up from below to form a background to their conversation – horns from the motor traffic, the clip-clop of horses' hooves from the ubiquitous gharries, occasional shouting matches between men in mock confrontation.

Sara was asking Gina about her work of interviewing Italian prisoners-of-war, because these accounts always astonished her.

'Honestly Sara, you couldn't make it up,' Gina was saying. 'I try to get the low-down out of them, but much of the time the

99

buggers are in tears, even the officers. I suppose no soldiers –
even the Germans – want be stuck out in the desert with people
taking pot-shots at them, but these Italians...they should be at
home with their mothers and girlfriends. They're obsessed with
mail from home. The fighting part – that's utterly foreign to
them. They don't have any aggressive feelings. It's just not
their thing.'

'It seems quite a nice quality in a way,' Sara began. 'Though I
suppose I shouldn't be saying that. I mean, what do you think
of these men? Do you like them?'

Gina shrugged. 'Oh well...they are a bit wet. *They* like *me*.
One of 'em asked me out last week. A prisoner-of-war!'

They both laughed.

'You know the Italian forces have prostitutes out in the
desert,' Gina said.

'Go on.'

'It's true. They're taken onto the strength of their units.'

Sara was fascinated. 'What about the British troops – how do
they manage out in the desert?'

'You're asking the wrong person. There's plenty of brothels in
Cairo, I do know that. They're in the Clot Bey area, north of
Ezbekieh Gardens.'

Sara looked up in astonishment. 'But that's not very far away.'

Gina grinned. 'No. Welcome to Cairo.'

'God Gina. I'm so incredibly ignorant about, you know...'

'About what?'

'Well, sex. Sexual matters. You wouldn't believe the things I don't know.'

Gina was laughing now. 'One day I'll tell you what *I* know. So far as it goes.' She stood up rather precariously on the balcony. 'Come on, let's go out on the town. Get your glad rags on. Tonight could be your lucky night, Sara Cox.'

They went to the branch of Groppi's in Adly Pasha Street where customers could sit out in a garden, and ate too much. Then on to the hotel Gina had found, complete with its dance floor. There was a decent band in residence, and more to the point a supply of decent young men of varying nationalities and occupations. The military ones were exclusively officers. The question of whether 'other ranks' would be allowed in didn't arise, because they couldn't have afforded it.

The girls had a couple of dances each, then sat on the sidelines drinking coffee, then returned to the fray. They never had long to wait for an invitation to dance. Sara stood smiling as she watched Gina sail onto the floor with an American officer. She became aware that someone was speaking to her.

'I think your friend is enjoying herself,' he said.

'She loves to dance,' Sara agreed.

She turned to have a proper look at the man who'd spoken. About the same height as her, dark hair, a darker shade of skin.

An Egyptian, to be sure, and with no trace of the bumptiousness that could afflict British officers in Cairo. She smiled in an automatic way, then took a closer look.

'I may have this completely wrong,' she said, 'But I feel we've met before.'

'I wish I *could* say we met,' he countered, 'But we were certainly in the same room. The Continental Hotel a few months ago. You danced with a British officer who trod on your toes.'

'You have an amazing memory.'

'I think that you remember too.'

For some reason – she didn't know why – her head was whirling. One immediate thought was that she mustn't refer to Paddy – the toe-treader – being in the SAS. They were constantly warned about loose talk with strangers and you never knew which side an Egyptian was on. Gina whirled past on the dance floor, grinning and raising her eyebrows appraisingly at the sight of Sara's companion.

'Yes,' she mumbled, 'I had to discourage that man to give my toes a rest.'

He laughed and held out a hand. 'Karim.'

'Sara.'

He told her he was a lawyer; that he worked for a firm which must have been important because even she had heard of it.

She told him she was a nurse at Helmieh Hospital. All the while they talked her thoughts were whirling. Not just her thoughts but her feelings too. Something was going on that she didn't understand. Her stomach fluttered uneasily, though they'd not eaten anything unusual at Groppi's. He asked how much she'd seen of Egypt and again she had to remind herself not to talk about the desert.

'I'm afraid it's mostly work,' she told him. 'And I've probably been inside too many hotels. Of course, I've seen the pyramids – who hasn't. A typical tourist.'

'Naturally the pyramids are interesting,' he replied, 'But you know the best thing about Cairo is the mosques. And unlike in many countries – Turkey, for instance – they're all different. And again unlike in other countries, an English woman can go inside them. You wouldn't do that in Baghdad – you'd never get out alive.'

'I didn't know that,' she managed to say, still ridiculously tongue-tied. She knew from the music that a new dance was beginning, and thought he would invite her onto the dance floor. He had other ideas.

'Please forgive me, Sara, if this is a bad suggestion. There is a well-known mosque in Cairo called Ibn Tulun. I think it is very beautiful. A place of peace. If you wanted to, I could take you there. Any time that's good for you.'

Sara's response was an absurd one of blind panic. She knew her face had gone beetroot red. He's an Egyptian, she was thinking. I'm being asked out by an Egyptian. Gina was by her side after her dance and gave Karim a friendly nod, but Sara stuttered in embarrassment.

'I'm sorry, but...no...thank you...I'm sorry.'

'You two go ahead,' Gina said, but Sara grabbed her arm and tried to move the two of them away.

'I am very sorry,' the Egyptian was saying. 'Please forgive me.' Composed, but clearly upset, he'd fallen back on good manners.

'Take no notice of her,' Gina told the man. 'She doesn't know what she's saying,' but Sara was already yards away. She literally ran to the ladies' cloakroom and locked herself in one of the cubicles.

When she emerged, Gina was waiting for her. 'We're going back to the flat,' she said. 'And you're going to tell me what's got into you.'

Gina was as good as her word. They took a gharry back to Garden City, then she sat Sara down at the dining room table and poured her a stiff drink. Gina sat opposite wagging a finger.

'I'm your friend, remember? So tell me, what was that ridiculous scene at the hotel about? That poor man you embarrassed. Why?'

'I don't...he...'

'Was it because he's Egyptian. Is that it? Are you xenophobic, or whatever? Do you only like British men?'

'No, no. I *don't* like British men.'

'What — *none* of them! For heaven's sake, Sara.'

'Please don't be angry with me. You *are* my friend, I know it. I'll tell you everything. You know all about men.'

'I know them, the buggers. But that Egyptian you talked to was all right, believe me.'

'It's like this.' Sara was calming down a bit now. She took a big gulp of whisky. 'I meet some men, yes, mostly British men. Sometimes they are quite nice. They are intelligent, maybe, or they treat me nicely, but...oh, this is so difficult.'

'Do you like women instead? Is that it?'

'What! No, no — of course not.'

'There's nothing wrong with women wanting women. That's the alternative to men.'

'Definitely not women. These men I meet...sometimes they want me, I can feel that, but I don't...I told you I'm ignorant about these things but I don't seem to want...'

'So OK, you're fussy. That's OK. A lot of women are. Don't understand it myself but...'

'Yes but this Egyptian man who I don't even know, this time I did feel...'

'You actually wanted him! Yes, that's how it happens. At last, we've got there. Hallelujah! My goodness, Sara, is that you smiling?'

'I may be.'

'OK, this is progress. Whew!' She picked up a fan off the table and waved it about her person. 'Now I'm beginning to get the picture.'

'Gina, please tell me everything. I mean everything *you* know about men.'

'How long have you got?'

'And I'm sorry I spoiled your evening. I mean, maybe you and your American dance partner, who knows...'

'Oh *him*. No, no, don't worry about that. He's from Texas. I have some standards.' She leapt to her feet. 'I'm going to make us some toast. If you keep knocking back the whisky like that I shall have to scrape you off the floor. We eat, and then I'll tell you what I know. Stay where you are.' She reached out to remove the whisky bottle.

Gina went to the flat's tiny kitchen, whence the aroma of toast and houmous began to emerge. Sara went to the bathroom and washed her face with cold water, then to the kitchen where she helped to make coffee. They ate, then took their coffee cups onto the balcony. The heat of the day had lifted and Gina put one of her cardigans over her friend's shoulders. Sara's body gave two involuntary shudders and Gina kissed the back of her neck. They sat in silence for several minutes watching the street below. A man wearing a red turban on his head rode the length of the street on a white horse. Gina reckoned her friend was calm enough to talk, and led her back to the table.

'So. If you like this Karim man and he likes you, what do you want to do about it?'

'I've actually been thinking about it...supposing that he and I are in bed together. I've never done that.'

'I thought maybe you hadn't.'

'If he wants me to, of course.'

'Oh he wants to. He'd give you a very nice time.'

'You think so? Do men know how to do that?'

'A lot of men are pig-ignorant. It's not their fault. But this Egyptian chap is quite mature. About 30 – what d'you think? And he's rich. That suit would have cost a fortune. He'll be experienced with women.'

'You mean young Egyptian women?'

'Good god, no. He couldn't lay a finger on them. I mean women he pays for.'

'In those brothels? Like the ones you said, in the Clot Bey area?'

'Of course not. Don't be daft, Sara. Top of the range women. Women who'll teach him how to give *them* pleasure.'

'Oh!'

'Don't look like that. How else is he going to learn?'

'It's all so complicated.'

Gina gave her friend a long look. 'So what else is bothering you?'

Sara returned the look, then took the plunge. 'The thing is, Gina, when a girl like me gets married, she's supposed to have kept her...you know, to be a...'

'A virgin. Of course. What d'you think *I* am?'

Sara stared. 'Then...forgive me, but how...?'

'Well there are ways and means. Some women who can afford it go to a very expensive kind of doctor. I've never been keen on needlework, so I just save that bit of myself for marriage.'

'But then how do the men...'

'Of course I don't know for sure because I haven't done it, but I can't imagine that intercourse – that's what we're talking about – can give more pleasure than a couple of knowing hands.' She waggled her fingers about. 'Or an adventurous mouth, for that matter. Why are you looking like that? Or even feet.'

'*What*!'

'You have nice feet. Some men like to be caressed by...now what?'

'Oh there's so much to learn. I'll never do it.'

'And there's kissing. We haven't even mentioned that. It's often described as the most intimate thing of all. They say that prostitutes won't even do it. You do kiss, I presume?'

Sara was looking anywhere but into her friend's eyes. 'I told you I was inexperienced.'

'I don't believe it.' Gina stood up from the table. 'You lop off men's limbs in the back of a lorry but you won't even kiss them. Come over here.'

'What! No...'

'Come here.'

Sara stood too, but stayed rooted to the spot. 'It's all right – I get the idea.'

'Come here.'

She did as she was told. Their mouths met. After a moment Sara made to pull away, but Gina held her tight. When they finally broke apart both girls were breathing heavily.

'Well, what do you think?' said Gina

'Yes, I do see. It was...it was really...oh...'

'And there's something else that we didn't even try. Did you think about doing it just then?'

'You mean...' Sara delicately poked the tip of her tongue out. 'Do people do that?'

'All the time.' Gina shook her head, as though trying to discourage a persistent wasp. 'We'd better stop now, or my long love affair with the opposite sex will be at risk. It's not just your nice looks, it's that deadly air of innocence...well, enough said. What are you going to do?'

'I'm not working tomorrow. Can I stay over?'

'You can stay as long as you like. You know that.'

'I'll try and find him tomorrow. And apologise.'

'Is that all?'

'We'll have to see.'

'I suppose that's something.'

*** *** ***

Next morning Sara left the flat straight after breakfast to search for the Egyptian she'd met the previous evening. All she knew was Karim's first name and the name – 'Mansour' – of the firm he worked for. She made for Shepheard's hotel and enquired at the information desk. A middle-aged Egyptian wearing an impressive peaked cap responded at once.

'Of course, miss. The firm is very well known. Ask anyone.'

He wrote down an address near Tahrir Bridge. It was no

distance from Shepheard's and she walked there alongside the river.

The law firm occupied the first two floors of an imposing-looking block. An expensively dressed young woman sat behind the reception desk. She spoke unusually good English.

'Can I help you?'

'I have a rather strange request,' Sara said.

'Try me.'

Sara said who she was and that she'd met a lawyer named Karim at a hotel the previous evening. By accident they'd become separated and now she needed to contact him.

The receptionist frowned. 'One of our lawyers does have that name. It could be him. But he is working from home today.'

'Can you give me his address?'

'As I'm sure you appreciate, this is difficult for me. I cannot give out our lawyers' addresses to anyone who calls in off the street.'

'I do understand,' Sara said. 'But I think he would want you to give it. He wants to take me to a mosque. He called it Ibn Tulun.'

Now the receptionist smiled. 'Yes, our Mr Mansour is a big enthusiast for mosques.' After a moment's thought she wrote on a sheet of the firm's headed paper. 'You can repeat your story to the security at his apartment block. I hope you are on the level, miss, or I shall be in trouble.'

'It will be fine. Thank you very much.'

The address was on the island of Zamalik, and not fancying the walk across one of the crowded bridges, Sara hailed a cab.

The security man at the next block was not immediately sympathetic, but jumped to it once he saw the note on the Mansour firm's headed paper. As he went to make enquiries, Sara remembered that the woman on reception had referred to 'Mr Mansour'. From the name and the way she said it, Sara realised that Karim Mansour was probably the firm's director.

A few minutes later she was in Karim's apartment. It stood on the top floor of the block, with spectacular views of the Nile on both sides of the island. The Cairo Tower was nearby.

Karim was casually dressed, sleeves rolled up, but it was clear he'd been working. Papers and reference books were strewn over a large desk. He waved at them dismissively. 'How wonderful to be interrupted.'

'I've come to apologise for yesterday,' Sara said.

'I'm the one to apologise. I upset you.'

'No. Forgive me, but that's not right. You were nice to me. I was like a stupid, spoilt child, and all because I thought you might like me. I have no experience with men and I panicked.'

'I think I *would* like you. I'd like the chance to find out.'

'I am here.'

'And I'm happy to see it. We need to talk, to spend time together, then perhaps we will know for sure.'

'That's fine, but there's something I want to get out of the way first. You don't know what a basket case I am about being with men...'

'Did you say *'Basket'*?'

'It's an expression. I've spent my entire life running away from men of all kinds. Until now I'd not met one who I wanted to...I mean, to...do you have a bed?'

'A bed! Of course. I sleep in it.'

'Please take me to it. I can't even think until...until we've...'

She took a few steps forward and pressed herself against him. After a moment he put his arms around her. She could feel her heart beating crazily, or was it his? Their heads were more or less level and she put her mouth carefully against his mouth. When he responded it felt even better than Gina's.

'A bed,' she repeated.

'Are you sure about this – it's very unusual.'

'Can we just see what happens?'

He looked dubious, but took her to a room with the most luxurious-looking bed she'd ever seen. Sara slipped out of her clothes as if she'd done it in front of a man many times before. She caught sight of her reflection in a mirror and thought she looked OK. Under the sheets he was tentative and extremely patient. He understood at once that she needed to keep her virginity. Between kisses she told him about herself, and he reciprocated. She thought they must have been in bed at least an hour before he introduced her to some things that were beyond her wildest imagination. She revelled in his body, and for the first time ever she found pleasure spreading across the whole of hers. She even wondered if her own unpractised gestures, the clumsy way she handled him, might be an acceptable contrast to what he was used to.

Yet another hour passed before their passion was sated, for the time being. She lay on her back and stretched luxuriously. Now starting to look for things to worry about – which was unlike her – she wondered if he might continue to seek her company only *because of* the sex.

'We are a strange couple,' she told him. 'I'm just a nurse in a Cairo hospital. You're the big boss in an important firm of lawyers.'

'It is indeed a strange contrast,' he replied. 'You are saving lives, which is the most valuable work anyone can do. Whereas my job is to put one man in a contest against another and charge ridiculous amounts of money for the privilege.'

She went quiet, but not for long. 'Yesterday evening you kindly offered to take me to a mosque,' she said. 'One day I would very much like to do that.'

He leapt up, pulling the covers off them both.

'How about now?'

He wouldn't listen to any protests about his work. They ate a snack in the kitchen, and within another 20 minutes they were out of the apartment. He owned a four year old Rover, and drove them to Cairo's Saiyida Zeinab area, where she'd never been before. They drew up in a street that featured an extraordinary congestion of buildings. A gang of small boys materialised from nowhere. Karim talked to one of them for a bit, then took Sara's arm and guided her away. The boy called after them.

'What did he say?' she asked.

'We were agreeing terms for him and his mates to guard the Rover. That last comment was "Not even one mosquito will land upon your vehicle, effendi".'

'What would happen if you didn't give him something?'

'Actually this one's a good lad,' he replied. 'But there's always the risk of finding your tyres let down.'

He handed over a cape to cover her head and shoulders, then led the way. For her the process of moving from the chaotic street into the mosque was like a conjuring trick. One moment everything was noise and confusion, whilst in the next the scene was utterly transformed. Karim said a few words to an attendant, to whom he was clearly well known, but offered no comment to Sara, merely standing back so that she could make her own discoveries. She was in a vast, square courtyard open to the elements except along the four sides, where a succession of columns supported a roof, affording narrow corridors of shade beneath. Columns after columns were visible for distances of well over a hundred metres. A small rounded construction in the centre of the square was all that broke up the acres of space. The sound effects had changed radically, from the raucous clatter of the street to a tranquil hum inside the mosque walls.

To her surprise Sara found she was crying, though she couldn't have explained why. Karim had not spoken, though she knew he was gratified by her reaction.

'Have you been into many Cairo mosques?' he asked at last.

She shook her head.

'Then if you like this...'

'Which you know I do.'

'...Perhaps I could take you to Qaitbay, in the City of the Dead. But there are also good things to see in the old city centre,' he went on mildly, and she imagined a hint of reproach in his voice. Not for the first time she thought of the hours she'd wasted in posh hotels.

Karim had told her that tourists visited Ibn Tulun and they spotted two other couples, though the mosque's size dwarfed every human presence. They traversed the covered walkways side by side, close but not touching. She felt composed and in no hurry to leave. All the same a renewed desire welled up in her body. 'Is this how it's going to be?' she wondered.

By the time they left, darkness was coming down – in unseemly haste, as always in Cairo. When he asked if she'd like

116

to eat something Sara found she was ravenous.

'Then let's dine,' he said.

She imagined he'd take her to some ritzy establishment, but not at all. They ate at a scruffy little café that served mouth-watering food. He told her some things about himself, but mostly he asked questions and listened. Afterwards what she really wanted to do was to climb all over him, but he began driving her back to Helmieh. She asked him to leave her at Gina's flat instead, because she knew her friend would want a report on the day. It happened that Gina was out (surprise, surprise). Sara scrawled a written account while Karim waited in the car. He seemed to have more reserves of patience than other men she'd known. Finally he deposited her at Helmieh, having first arranged for them to meet again.

That night she fell asleep with difficulty, wondering how long she could hold this surprising interloper, and how he could be accommodated in her life.

Over the next few months Sara found herself ill-prepared for a relationship that demanded her time on a regular basis. At the best of times Helmieh nurses worked long hours, and she could never expect the flexibility that Karim enjoyed in his own organisation. Helmieh was busier than ever. British troops in North Africa were increasingly preoccupied with Rommel's Germans, and as the war went badly so more and more casualties were transferred to British hospitals.

Sara immediately discontinued her visits to Cairo hotels, but was determined to keep up with Gina, who had always been so kind to her. The practicalities of making arrangements and rearranging them during emergencies caused endless problems in a chaotic place like Cairo. When Sara and Karim needed to change plans, it was usually necessary for one of them to travel the 15 kilometres between Helmieh and central Cairo. Over time Karim's capable receptionist became Sara's friend and confidante. But then the Indonesian nurse Rose, who shared Sara's tent, often fielded messages from Karim. Gina's flat, too, proved to be a useful location for posting communications. Sara introduced Gina to Karim one evening and he took the pair of them out to dinner.

Sara found it best not to brood on the future with her lover because she knew there couldn't be one. He told her that he had so far warded off his parents' attempt to fit him up with a wife, but sooner or later he'd be spoken for. One afternoon Sara was invited to tea with 'the mother', a rather gloomy woman whose husband had been 'out of town'. Sara didn't know if Karim had other girlfriends and she didn't ask. She did speculate as to why he spent so much time with an ingenuous young woman like her; whether, consummate English speaker that he was, he had ambitions to incorporate more expressions like 'basket case' into his lexicon, or whether it was the novelty of tasting innocent young flesh, albeit not fucking it (a word Sara found herself dwelling upon more often than before).

Cairo's multi-national, multi-religious population was a hot-bed of gossip, and Karim's own observations helped to amplify Sara's sketchy grasp of local politics. Of course she'd been aware (who couldn't be?) that the British were unpopular in

118

Egypt, and that Egyptians resented Britain, Germany and Italy fighting a war on their territory, but the finer details had eluded her. The advent of war had punched holes in what was once a workable treaty between Britain and Egypt. That treaty gave Britain the right to defend Egypt against attack, but also the right for Egypt to manage its own affairs, something which the British constantly flouted. The machinations between King Farouk, the British ambassador, Sir Miles Lampson, and Prime Minister Ali Pasha were central to much of the gossip. Some stories were so irresistible that they went round Cairo like a forest fire. Until Karim told her about it, Sara seemed to be the only person in the capital who hadn't heard that Lampson's wife was half-Italian, and Farouk had remarked 'I won't get rid of my Italians till he gets rid of his'. More seriously, Lampson had arranged for the ousting of Prime Minister Ali Maher. Worse still were the events of February 1942, when Lampson engineered the installation of a new government under the Wafd Party – and very nearly the expulsion of King Farouk himelf. Through Karim, Sara got to know about these things soon after they occurred.

Of course what everyone wanted to know was the progress of the war – not hyped-up propaganda stories peddled by the warring parties, but realistic appraisals of the situation. By any measure things didn't go well for the British in June 1942 when Rommel captured the port of Tobruk then, drove further east into Egypt to take Mersa Matruh. He finally halted near a little known railway town called el Alamein, a mere 60 miles from Alexandria. The bleak situation attracted notice when German radio broadcast a message to Alexandria's women: 'Get out your party frocks, girls, we're on the way'. It was less well known that Germany's troops were drained from weeks of fighting, and Rommel's 1,000-mile supply line from Tripoli had become dangerously stretched.

~ Six ~

Johnny, July 1942

Receiving her mother's first letter had been a significant event for Sara. It stimulated a flood of her own letters, so that despite the attentions of the local censor she could unburden herself to the one person she was closest to. Once they started, her mother's letters arrived more often and contained increasingly lucid information.

The third letter from home contained a big surprise. Sara's only cousin, the son of her mother's brother, had been posted to Egypt on military service and was likely to be in Cairo already. He was a young man called Johnny, a couple of years older then Sara herself. She'd known he was in training at the military barracks in Aldershot and now it seemed he'd been assigned to a tank regiment. The news astonished her. For months she'd been alone in Cairo, a young girl amongst strangers, and seeing a familiar face would be hard to take on board. It was not an unmixed blessing. Her days were spent helping to patch up wounded British soldiers, and the best element of this was that she didn't have feelings for any of them. The thought of ministering to someone she knew didn't appeal at all. That said, she soon realised that Johnny's presence in Cairo would give her a lift. In her recollection he was a young man with a distinctly likeable personality.

The immediate problem was how to contact the lad. No doubt her mother would have given Johnny a clue to Sara's whereabouts – 'a tent somewhere in Helmieh', she thought with a grin – but if she knew Johnny he'd wait until *she* got in touch with *him*. This was easier said than done. Like most girls in her position she had little or no contact with private soldiers socially. (Medically, as in a hospital – yes, sadly that was another matter.)

The difficulty was solved by Gina. Gina had a contact – she always did – and said that once she had Johnny's full name it should be easy to track him down. She was as good as her word. She handed over a location, along with a time that Johnny had agreed to be around. For good measure she offered to go along too. Sara resisted the urge to tease her friend – that after working her way through Britain's officer cadre she wanted to explore other ranks – and reflected that the Italian girl's easy manner would help to break the ice.

Pondering on what to take Johnny she rejected the notion of beer, which he'd have too much of already, and settled on a very large box of Huntley & Palmer biscuits, an echo of provisions from home that was available from Cairo stores. For good measure she added a bottle of whisky.

The two girls took a cab to the Almaza military camp, arriving soon after dark. They were surprised to find a gathering of Egyptians in the nondescript patch of ground outside the camp. As far as they could tell the reason for this presence was the locals wanting to see what a bunch of British soldiers got up to in their spare time.

122

It was the first time either girl had witnessed the kind of facilities used by other ranks, and they weren't impressed. The camp seemed to contain a multitude of square-shaped tents and very little else. Gina had fixed it so they met Johnny in the bar, another depressing sight that offered little beyond some wooden tables and an old refrigerator. And it was there, with a pang, that Sara saw him, looking absurdly young, grinning all over his face, lounging against a table amongst a bunch of his mates. Fortunately both she and Gina had dressed down for the occasion, but she was at once aware of the lads' eyes boring into them, as if they hadn't seen a woman for weeks on end. She cast caution aside and forged in amongst them to embrace her cousin, causing the others to give a raucous cheer. She felt absurdly emotional and raised one hand to brush away a tear.

'Johnny, I can't believe this,' she cried.

'Nor can I,' was all he would say.

He wasn't a bloke who was used to making introductions, but he waved at the others, who crowded round. Sara put an arm round Gina's waist.

'This is my very good friend, Gina. She's half Italian.' More cheers.

Gina cried out, to laughter 'Hello boys. It's great to see you living in such a luxury hotel.' She was entirely at easy in their ribald company.

By degrees they sorted themselves out. It soon became clear that the lads were members of Johnny's tank crew. The most senior one, a sergeant called George, was older than the others and a bit more serious. It was George who eventually introduced everyone.

Sara bought drinks all round and handed over the bottle of whisky, but the Huntley & Palmer biscuits proved to be the big attraction. Johnny ripped open the box straight away and she saw how this small reminder of home affected them.

'It's a funny thing,' said Johnny, 'But I was thinking of biscuits as I tried to eat my horrible breakfast this morning.' At once Sara remembered that 'It's a funny thing', was one of several such phrases that littered Johnny's conversation. It was a mannerism that defined him. The others had got used to it too, because one of them repeated 'Is it a funny thing, Johnny?', not sarcastically but in a nice way – he was clearly popular – and Johnny came back with 'Yes, it is a *really* funny thing.'

It took a while but they settled down eventually. George the sergeant pushed a couple of tables together and the conversation became more reflective. They were nice boys, far from home, and the smallest thing aroused their interest. Sara realised how much she was enjoying their company. There was a great gulf between these lads and the officer class she'd foolishly spent so much time with. She started to buy a second round of drinks but Gina objected and stepped up to the bar herself, amidst cheers. Six pairs of eyes hungrily followed her elegant figure as she moved across the grotty little bar space.

'So I suppose you sleep in those square tents we saw,' said Sara as Gina rejoined them.

124

'All in the same one,' said Johnny. 'Eight men to a tent.'

'Do you have camp beds?' Gina enquired.

'Nothing like that,' said another lad. 'On the ground. We use our boots for pillows.'

Sara's thoughts went back to the night-time arrangements with the SAS, though they at least had sleeping bags. She thought it better not to mention the SAS experience.

When it was quieter she asked 'What's it like being in a tank? I mean, do you blokes feel safe?'

Automatically the others looked to George for a reply. 'If you compare it to the infantry lads walking beside a tank,' he said, 'Then you're glad to have the protection of being inside. Though we wish our machines were as tough as those Kraut affairs. But if you're hit, and you brew up...' He whistled and clapped his hands. 'Different story.'

'What does it mean, this "brew up"?' Gina asked.

'It's when there's a fire in the tank,' George explained. The others had gone quiet. 'Thing is, in a tank you're surrounded by combustibles. There's the petrol in the engine. You've got ammunition all round the turret.'

'So what do you do if the tank brews up?' asked Sara.

'You've got five seconds,' George said. 'It's longer than you think.'

'So...?'

'Oh, I jump out first, of course. The army values its sergeants.' He waved towards the others, amidst laughter. 'Never mind this no-good crowd.'

'It's a funny thing,' said Johnny, and they started describing tanks they'd seen brewing up. All the same that moment's silence had given Sara pause for thought.

Later on when they were quieter, talking in ones and twos, she had a few minutes alone with her cousin.

'Are you OK?' she asked.

'Yeah, I'm all right.' He looked so innocent, so fragile, standing in a crude bar many miles from home; she simply couldn't connect him to being behind a gun in a tank, killing Germans. He wasn't the sort of lad who analysed issues and formed opinions. The here and now was his world. 'Could do with some better grub,' he said, substantiating her unspoken thoughts. 'They tell you, whatever you do don't touch an Egyptian sausage. *Avoid the sausage.* I ate one once by mistake. Spent two days on the toilet. And you haven't seen the toilets.'

Sara was thinking that all over North Africa there'd be young men like Johnny sent out to war, firing guns or being fired at, not knowing why they were there, maybe not even knowing for sure where they were.

She nodded towards the others, who were drooping half-sozzled over the tables. 'They seem like a nice bunch.'

He waved at two of the lads, who waved back. 'They're a laugh, aren't they.'

'I expect you see a lot of them?'

'Course I do – they're my crew. It's like, your home. Long as you're with your crew there's people who know you and look out for you. You have a laugh. It's a funny thing but without your crew you're nothing. Like when you first arrive...' He broke off to gesticulate to his mates. 'Oi, leave some of them biscuits for me, you lot.'

Around nine o'clock Sara thought she and Gina ought to get moving. She told Johnny she'd like to take him to Groppi's the following week. 'It's a famous restaurant, Johnny. Really good food.'

'No sausages?'

'Not a sausage in sight. I'll come and pick you up in a gharry. You might find that interesting. Same time, eh?'

She hailed a cab to take herself and Gina back to Garden City.

'What did you think?' she asked Gina in the back of the cab.

'I enjoyed it. Nice boys.'

'Yeah.'

Several minutes passed before Gina spoke again.

' I wouldn't want to be in a tank that brewed up.'

'No, me neither.'

***   ***   ***

A few days later Sara lunched with Karim in a restaurant near his office. As he paid the bill, he told her he needed to visit the Anglo-Egyptian Union. Sara had never heard of it.

'The nice thing about it is the garden,' Karim said. 'Lots of really lovely trees. A good spot to sit around in.'

'And the not nice thing?'

'I'm afraid there *is* something you might not like. The place has become a sort of centre for literary people. They can be a bit stuffy.'

'Do they bite?'

He laughed. 'Not as bad as that.'

'Then can I come with you?'

'I was hoping you'd say that.'

The club – in Sharia Fuad el Awad – was just as he'd said. Trees towered above a grassy area where members sat at tables and were served by waiters. A little world of its own. Karim took them first to the office, where he collected a magazine called *Personal landscapes.* Then on to one of the tables where they drank glasses of a hibiscus tea called karkadeh. He took a quick look at the magazine before putting it in his briefcase.

'Don't you have to pay for that?' Sara enquired. 'It looked as if they just gave it to you.'

'Nothing escapes you, does it. It's a literary magazine. I had a couple of pieces in it, so I get a free copy.'

'A couple of pieces. May I see?'

He took *Personal landscapes* out again and turned to a page that contained two short poems by Karim Mansour. She read them through, then read them again.

'I may be wrong,' she said, 'But one of these...'

'Was inspired by you, that's right. You were my muse.'

'So you're a writer. A writer who's been published, but you didn't think to tell me.'

'My stuff is nothing really. I'm the tame Egyptian. I'm tolerated by the bigger luminaries.'

'I like your stuff, as you call it.'

Before he could respond a man approached their table and apologised for interrupting. 'I'm sorry, my dear,' he told Sara, clapping Karim on the shoulder. 'Just wanted to congratulate this man on his work. He's very good, you know.'

'Is he?'

'Don't let him tell you otherwise. He knocks the rest of us into a cocked hat. Sorry to butt in.' He hurried away.

'Who was that?' she asked, when the interloper was out of earshot.

'His name's Lawrence Durrell. He was one of the three men who started this *Personal landscapes* enterprise.'

'And is he one of the...the luminies...whatever you said?'

'I think he may come to be one.' Karim gazed at Durrell's retreating back. 'These poor devils. Because of the war they've all fetched up in Cairo, where they try to scratch a living. Lawrence is teaching at the American university here. He's written a first novel called *Pied piper of lovers*. Says the sales haven't funded a ham sandwich.'

'He seemed to think highly of your work.'

'It's kind of him.'

'So would you describe yourself as a poet?'

'That's complicated. People who write poetry are schoolteachers, accountants, engineers night-club bouncers...lawyers.'

'Now you're teasing me.'

'I think maybe I'm a poet at the moment I actually write down the lines.'

'So it doesn't mean anything to you – being a poet?'

'I didn't say that. If I could only do law I'd go mad. I'd be gibbering. A world without the arts would be a grim place.'

'So it's important to you?'

He shrugged.

'But you didn't think to tell me.'

'People don't always talk about the important things. I know a nurse who carried out a very difficult operation in the back of a lorry. Saved a man's life. She never talks about it.'

Sara felt colour rise into her face. She wished it wouldn't do that. 'Has *anything* happened that you don't know about?' she said.

'Lots of things.'

'What I don't know would fill the world's biggest encyclopaedia. I'm sitting in this nice place amongst all these...'

'Luminaries.'

'Yes, them, and what I especially don't know is literature.'

'It's all ahead of you.'

'You think so?'

'I'm sure of it.'

'Is there someone here whose books I should read?'

'It's not so obvious. You see that couple over there.' He

131

pointed to a young couple sitting 20 yards away. The man was talking expansively, waving his arms about. The young woman lolled back in her chair looking bored. 'His name is Reggie Smith. A really nice man. Tremendously well informed about literature. He teaches at the university too.'

'And the woman? She looks like she could be a pain in the neck.'

He grinned. 'I don't know that expression but yes, that has been said. Her name's Olivia.'

'So she's just tagging along?'

'Actually she's writing a novel. People who've seen it say it's going to be very good. *She's* the writer.'

'That's it. I give up.'

'Don't do that. Just make a start. Take it one thing at a time.'

'Then tell me something to read. Anything.'

He bent down to his briefcase again and took out a book. 'Thomas Hardy. Poet.'

'Never heard of him.'

'Now you have. Died a dozen years ago. Still has some things to say to our generation.'

'What – like he writes about war?'

'Well, not sure about that. He loves grave-stones though.

They're his favourite things.'

'Weird.'

'War, hm...hold on a minute.' He leafed through the book.
'Yes, here we are. It's about the little creatures who live in the
ground and what will happen to them during the battle of
Waterloo. I believe that was one of your country's big battles.'

'Even I've heard of it.'

'Here we go.' He read from the poem.

> *'The snail draws in at the terrible tread*
>
> *But in vain. He is crushed by the wheel's rim.*
>
> *The worm asks what can be overhead*
>
> *And wriggles deep from a scene so grim,*
>
> *And guesses him safe; for he does not know*
>
> *What a foul red tide will be soaking him...*

And so on.'

'It's amazing.'

'That's poetry for you. You're on your way. Here, take it with
you.' He handed the book across the table.

'I can't do that.'

'I want you to have it.'

She turned the book over in her hands as though it was some foreign object. 'Thank you. Thank you very much. I'm on my way.'

~ Seven ~

The battle of Alamein, October 1942

Sara was always to link that first meeting with cousin Johnny to the approach of battle. War was the subject on everyone's mind. It was evident in the movements of troops and vehicles. Its flavour was in the dust that settled on every surface. The notion of conflict had a lot to do with the proximity of gathering forces. Of course the north African conflict had been grinding on for nearly two years, but now German troops (and Italian, for that matter) were assembling on Cairo's own doorstep. Conversation amongst the British community rarely focussed on anything else, and because of her link with Karim Sara knew that Egyptians were similarly obsessed. Locals could imagine the Germans sweeping down from the Delta regions into the capital, with unpredictable consequences. There was excitement, but also fear. Nothing was certain.

Sara kept her Groppi's date with Johnny, which went better than expected. She'd noticed her cousin's difficulties with the local food, but he took a liking to Groppi's' famous pastry and finished his meal with two helpings of cream cakes.

A curious thing happened as the two of them sat in the Groppi's garden scoffing their grub. A British officer stopped at their table and said 'Hello' – causing Johnny to leap up and salute. Sara recognised the man immediately; it was Lieutenant

Harness, the Scotsman who'd looked after her at the Turf Club during her first ever sally into Cairo society. She felt him to be one of the more decent men she'd encountered in that phase of her life. She stood up to talk, while Johnny resumed his seat.

'Sorry not to have seen you recently,' Harness told her. 'Heard about your exploits though. Back of a lorry and all that.'

Sara suppressed a sigh. It seemed nothing was sacred in the Cairo gossip machine. To get her own back she mentioned something about *him*. 'I remember you telling me that Wavell would be losing his job, despite his record of success – and you were proved right.'

Harness put a finger to his lips. 'WSC is nothing if not impatient. I fear it's going to happen again.'

'What do you mean?'

He glanced at all the people sitting around and lowered his voice. 'You know there's just been a battle at Alam Halfa?'

'We heard something. News is filtering through.'

'It was an impressive victory for Auchinleck, though you wouldn't believe it, hearing some of the talk.' He spoke even more quietly. 'The Auk will suffer the same fate as Wavell. Then there's going to be an even bigger fracas – a final one – under a new general.'

'So who will replace...'

Harness glanced around. He knew he shouldn't, but couldn't

136

resist it. 'There's a bloke called Montgomery. Stand by your beds.'

'You don't sound very keen.'

'Mum's the word.'

He walked away without acknowledging Johnny.

By an extraordinary coincidence Sara caught sight of 'The Auk' (as Auchinleck was known) soon afterwards. She was dining with Karim on the terrace of Mena House, a restaurant he'd been keen to introduce her to. As they were finishing their starters two British men in lounge suits sat down at a nearby table. Karim took a quick look then leant across the table to whisper.

'The man on the right is Sir Claude Auchinleck. He's just been relieved of the command of British forces in Egypt.'

'Who's the other chap?' she whispered back.

'I think that's one of his officers called Dorman Smith. Bit of a dubious character.'

'You only *think*! You're slipping.'

'The grape-vine is not always reliable.'

With the prospect of a battle – and a possible German victory – so close, Gina chose this moment to cajole Sara into visiting Alexandria. Neither girl had been to Egypt's second city, and with the conflict approaching it seemed like a case of now or never. The train to Alex took an hour and a half. They went up on Saturday, slept on the floor of a house owned by one of Gina's friends, and planned to return on Sunday morning. As soon as they'd arrived, both girls were glad they'd made the effort. The contrast between Cairo and the cosmopolitan Alexandria struck them most forcibly. Early Saturday evening they were sitting in one of the cheap brasseries on the Corniche enjoying a dish of kleftika and listening to a Greek chanteuse, whose dress was a flimsy affair that would never have passed muster in the capital. The sight and sound and smell of the sea pervaded the atmosphere. After Cairo the town seemed very liberated, but 'freedom' was a notional concept with the Germans so near. There were signs that some of the population were on their way out. They saw heavily laden cars leaving the city for an uncertain fate in the Delta region. Air raid sirens were a regular feature, though Gina had been assured that attacks were concentrated in the harbour area. The girls were excited by the air of frenetic activity, but the image that dominated Sara's thoughts was that of an out-of-control train rushing pell-mell for the buffers.

When Sara was back in Cairo the clearest indication of military jitters came via a summons to see Matron, something that had happened only once before, when she was recruited by the SAS. She went to Matron's office and was told to sit down.

'I have something serious to discuss with you,' the woman said.

'Yes Matron.'

'You're an intelligent girl. You'll be aware that there's talk of a major battle in the offing at Alamein.'

'I heard something.'

'If it goes as expected there will be a great many British casualties. They've got a new man in charge who's a stickler for preparation. It seems they're all right for stretcher-bearers and ambulance drivers, but they're desperately short of doctors and nurses. I've been asked if we can help. Do you know what a RAP is?'

'Regimental Aid Post, Matron.'

'That's correct. It's the first place a casualty is taken by a stretcher-bearer. From there he goes to a Casualty Clearing Station or a field hospital. The point is, a RAP is very close to the action. Do you understand?'

Sara felt a tingle of excitement and fear. 'Yes Matron. I'd like to help.'

'Perhaps I haven't made myself clear. This is a dangerous place to be. Your SAS job was simple by comparison.'

'I'd like to help, Matron, if you will agree.'

The Matron let slip a cluck of irritation. 'Nurse Cox, you are a very foolhardy girl.' To Sara's amazement the woman advanced and levelled a sort of peck at her forehead. Her aim was poor; probably she hadn't kissed anyone for many years.

'All right then,' she said in a strangled sort of voice. 'I'll put your name forward. Good luck.'

*** *** ***

Sara's first thought about the forthcoming battle was that Johnny would be involved in it. She called in at his camp one evening to wish him luck but he wasn't about, so she had to leave a note. She sent best wishes, then wrote that she was also likely to be involved in the battle, on the medical side. Two days later she was astonished to return to her Helmieh tent and find that Johnny had called by, spoken to Rose, and left *her* a note wishing *her* luck. She was touched that he'd gone to such trouble, which was unusual for him, and wished she'd been present when he called.

Her meeting with Matron soon brought results. On 20th October she was ordered to convene, along with other nurses and a few doctors, at Cairo's General Hospital. From there this group of some 30 people was driven in a tourist bus and deposited in a decrepit guest house on the western outskirts of Alexandria. Few of her fellow-medics were in talkative mood and the journey passed in near-silence. At the guest house they were told to stay inside, to avoid letting slip information (information they didn't have!) and to await further instructions. Over the next two days the group met at meal times, where they exchanged desultory speculation about what was to happen. None of them had been present at a battle before. Every so often Sara peered out of the window to

140

observe the soldiers posted at intervals around the building – whether to keep the medics from going out or outsiders from coming in was unclear.

She'd wondered about the intricacies of planning for war. Clearly the military would want their medics on hand at the outset of hostilities, but she failed to see how the start of a battle could be precisely anticipated. In the event they were only cloistered in the guest house for two days, before a fleet of ambulances turned up to convey them 60 miles to a spot near Alamein. After that it became pretty clear, from the intense military activity on the British side, that something was about to go off.

Her first RAP site was within the sound (but not sight) of the Mediterranean. She remembered Paddy telling her 'Nearly all the actual fighting takes place within 60 miles of the coastal road'. From the start Sara had the impression the Regimental Aid Posts were short of staff. The one she joined started off with two doctors and two nurses, including herself. They were promised another nurse, who never arrived, and as events unfolded soon found themselves hard pressed. There was no way of knowing whether the staff shortage was a function of military planning or an unexpected surfeit of casualties – or simply a scarcity of medical personnel.

For a while her RAP group made their preparations near to where a battalion of the Durham Light Infantry was preparing for action. As things turned out this meant that very early on Sara clapped eyes on Montgomery, the new commander everyone was talking about (and whose name she'd first heard indiscreetly murmured by Lieutenant Harness in Groppi's restaurant). Montgomery had called by to address a section of the battalion, well within earshot of Sara's RAP group. Naturally the medics stopped whatever they were doing to listen in.

'He's known for these pep talks,' observed Dr Stirling, a man in his fifties who looked as if he might need medical attention himself.

'What do you make of him?' asked the other chap, a doctor named Wragg.

'Bit of a sly-boots. Spins a good line.'

'They say he's popular with the men.'

'Mm.'

They stood and watched as Montgomery finished his pep talk. He didn't look like any other general Sara had seen; indeed was quite unlike the giant Auchinleck whom she'd briefly spotted in the Mena House restaurant. Montgomery was a small man with a rather strutting manner of moving about. He wore the black beret for which he was already famous, and which helped to distinguish him from other officers. When he saluted it was done with an enormous flourish. He eventually moved on somewhere else, and a group of soldiers from his audience came within earshot of the RAP group.

'That's the first time I've ever been told what I was supposed to do in a battle,' said one of them.

'The bloke seems to be organised – I'll give him that,' said a second man.

'I know what you mean,' his companion replied. 'I'll go into battle for him, dammit.'

Like it or not, these men *would* be going into battle, and soon. Shortly before 10pm on the evening of 23 October, hundreds of British guns began to fire over the Axis front line. The noise of the barrage was unlike anything Sara had experienced. 'I'll be hard put to describe this to mum next time I write home,' was the thought that occurred to her. The entire skyline turned red under the bombardment. Their little RAP group could only sit and watch, since no form of speech would have prevailed against such a din. After some 20 minutes the bombardment was lifted. For a moment the silence seemed wonderful and they were able to distinguish stars in the sky. Yet Sara knew that thousands of men would now be advancing towards the Axis lines, moving in their steady, deliberate manner while the shells rained down upon them. She felt grateful to have been born a woman, immune from exposure to such jeopardy.

The medics had to stop being fascinated onlookers and start doing their job, because wounded men arrived as soon as the barrage was lifted. They were not the sort of casualties she dealt with at Helmieh Hospital – the cleaned up figures, injuries neatly dressed, arriving with descriptions of their problems attached. Here in Alamein the wounded were picked up by the stretcher-bearers and delivered to RAP groups stationed beyond the fray, where they were assessed and patched up, then loaded onto meat-wagons (the soldiers' unvarying term for ambulances) for delivery to the nearest field hospital. There would be no amputations in the back of a lorry in this place. Her job was to stop bleeding, treat for shock, put on dressings and murmur encouraging words.

The RAP group worked in the open, on an undulating patch of desert and scrub illuminated by the indispensable Hurricane lamps. Dust and sand drifted across the scene as they laboured. The wounded men were anxious, groaning, crying out, spluttering and coughing from the residue of bursting shells. Soldiers and medics alike smelt blood and the acrid odour of cordite, and all too often the sweet smell of death. Sara had met these injuries before in Helmieh. She knew about shell splinters and land-mines, bullets, bayonet wounds, burns from 'brewed up' tanks. She knew that a lump of shrapnel made a bigger hole coming out of the human body that it did going in. Yet the immediacy of her present situation gave the work a very different focus.

The medics worked individually, with little co-ordination between them. They'd barely spoken to each other. At some point the older doctor disappeared, leaving just Dr Wragg and the two nurses.

After hours of toil Sara realised that her movements were becoming automatic, that she she was no longer thinking straight. The problems appeared before her and she responded like an automaton. She knew this wasn't good enough. Soldiers were individuals, who reacted differently to adversity. The few words a nurse might exchange with a wounded man could make an important contribution to his morale. She made an effort to do better. She'd devised her own rule for these delicate

144

situations, namely never to lie to a patient about his condition, except when she knew he was going to die. She doubted whether her Helmieh Matron would have approved.

A nagging worry was that her clothes were soaked in blood. She could feel its viscous consistency on her thighs. It went against all medical protocols to allow one person's blood to mingle with another's, but the stuff was everywhere – on her gloved hands, on her clothes and skin, all over the ground, pumping from the bodies of the wounded beyond any control.

Time seemed to have lost its meaning at Alamein. She'd been working for hours when a Medical Officer appeared on the scene – an older man with an authoritative manner. He needed to grasp Sara's arm before she became aware of his presence.

'Thank you, nurse,' he told her. 'You've done well, but you need a break.'

'I can go on if you need someone,' she said, in headless chicken mode.

'No you cannot. You're all in.'

'I've never done this before.'

He asked her name and said she was being relieved, then took her arm and personally led her to an ambulance. She was driven a short distance to some tents reserved for doctors and nurses to rest. They were like crude versions of the tent she inhabited at Helmieh. She was given a clean uniform and told to put her blood-stained garment in a bin. A crude open-air shower area allowed her to sponge the blood from her body. Inside the tent were sleeping forms. There was just enough light for Sara to find a sleeping bag and climb into it. The moment she put her head down, oblivion descended.

She woke to find a woman shaking her roughly by the shoulders. Light was streaming into the tent.

'Come on, miss,' the woman said. 'It's ten o'clock. Time for work.'

An awning had been set up outside, with tables and chairs underneath. Several people were there, including Dr Wragg and the other nurse of her group. They acknowledged her but seemed otherwise barely conscious. There were cups of tea, rolls and some biscuits.

Within 30 minutes of rising she was back on duty – possibly in the same spot, though the change from darkness to light made it hard to tell. They relieved three other people, who gratefully moved away. The air was thick with smoke. The sound of war battered their ears. There was urgent activity in the immediate vicinity – people running back and forth, stretcher-bearers, ambulances. In the harsh light of morning all these details took on a cruder aspect.

In short order Sara and the other two were back to routines familiar from the previous night: the pitiless conveyor belt of the wounded, the dying and the dead, the relentless staunching of blood, patching up, cheerful words in a cheerless setting. As before, the medics barely had time to communicate with each other.

Amidst it all Sara found her thoughts straying back to the interview with Matron at Helmieh. 'Nurse Cox, you are a very foolhardy girl,' Matron had said in her frustration. The old bat had known what lay in store for her charge and tried to restrain her from volunteering. She supposed that Matron was 'sweet on her', in the phrase commonly used; it happened sometimes in an all-female environment. The woman had wanted to to save her from a traumatic experience, but no – I wanted this, Sara thought, I insisted. Ever since my friendship with Penny at the London Hospital I've wanted it. I rush blindly into things and must now stick them out; either that, or run home with my tail between my legs.

With more time to reflect, she'd have realised that every encounter with a wounded man was changing her in small ways. She found that ordinary soldiers revealed more of themselves than the officer class. A dying man often talked of his mother, in terms that brought tears to even a nurse's beady eyes. For most wounded soldiers their first request was a cigarette, and even non-smokers would light up a fag. She formed a clearer picture of what it was like being out there. One man told her you couldn't see more than 40 yards ahead. Another said it was like being drunk. She'd not realised there were men used to 'count the paces', so their officer would know the platoon's distance from the enemy front line. One of these young 'counters', who would not survive his injuries, continued to murmur the numbers as his life's blood drained away. Other men referred to Montgomery's obsession with minor details, which had made an impression on them. The sergeant of a tank crew – of course, she thought of Johnny – said he'd insisted that no turret lid could be closed during an attack. She found that all the soldiers, whether or not they were Scottish, liked to hear the pipes that accompanied the Highland regiments. She too had heard the strains of pipes borne upon the wind. There were pipers amongst the wounded.

Of course Sara and her RAP colleagues dealt with men who were – at least for a time – still alive. She saw the other side of the coin when a British truck passed close to where they were working. One glance revealed that the vehicle was full of dead bodies. It stank horribly.

Sara hadn't entered into the Alamein experience with any deep knowledge of battles and she'd no idea how long this one was likely to last. The daily pattern of events seemed much like what had gone before. The second day was like the first. The third day was like the second. There was no let-up in the numbers of men she had to treat. In the middle of her fourth day something unbelievable happened, because there was a lull in the numbers of wounded being ferried back to the RAP. The hiatus lasted barely half and hour yet brought relief. Her fellow nurse was in no state to take advantage of it; she sat down away from her companions and stared at the ground. But Dr Wragg moved towards Sara and held out a hand.

'James Wragg.'

Sara reciprocated. 'Sara Cox.'

Later these introductions seemed unreal, following as they did four days of working in close proximity, but that was how it happened.

By a happy chance the tea wagon passed by at this moment and brought them cups of tea.

'Sorry we've had no chance to talk,' Wragg said. 'What do you make of all this?'

'It's beyond my wildest imagining,' Sara admitted.

Wragg nodded. Despite the non-stop pressure he looked like a man whose brain was still active. 'I'm not surprised. You've done very well.'

'Thank you.'

He gazed into the distance, where sounds of conflict continued. 'You know, there's something wrong here.'

'What do you mean?'

'Well...look, I'm a bit of a military history buff.' (This turned out to be an understatement.) 'Of course, back here we don't get to know what's going on. Even in command posts the state of a battle can be hard to read. But by now the British should have broken through the Axis front line.'

'Why do you say that?'

He gave her an appraising look. 'Do you know the sort of numbers involved?'

'I know next to nothing.'

'Of course – there's no reason why you should know. The point is, the British have a massive numerical advantage.'

'I see.'

'Naturally neither side will be bandying the numbers about. They'll keep mum. But we've got – I don't know – at least 200,000 men in the field. Maybe more.'

'Blimey! And the Germans?'

'Well the Axis have about half that. 100,000 maybe. Only half of them are German, the rest Italian.' He looked up at the sky. 'And also, by the way, we've got complete control of the air. As I say, we really should have broken through by now.'

'Then it should be a piece of cake,' Sara said.

Wragg pursed his lips. 'War doesn't work like that, sadly. All the same...we must have messed up somehow.'

'What I keep thinking,' Sara said, 'Is what a terrible waste...I mean of people.'

'Oh Montgomery's not worried about that sort of thing. For him soldiers are pawns to be moved about. He's well known for it.'

'But surely...'

'After all, he's not out on the battlefield himself, is he? That first night, when our first wave of men went over, he was tucked up in bed asleep.'

She stared at him.

'These things leak out,' he said. 'Sorry to bang on at you. It's something I feel strongly about.'

'What about tanks?' she asked, thinking here was a man who knew his stuff. 'Are we all right for them? I've got a cousin in one somewhere out there.'

'I hope he's all right,' said Wragg. 'He'll have a good chance. We've got an enormous advantage in tanks, including nearly 300 Shermans. But fingers crossed, eh? There are no certainties.'

'I suppose..' she began hesitantly. 'I mean they've got this Rommel chap, haven't they. He's supposed to be the best.'

'No, no, no.' Wragg's rejoinder was vehement. 'Rommel's sick. He's in a hospital, god knows where. Not in north Africa, anyway. Oh dear!' He pointed straight ahead. 'Do you see what I see?'

Sure enough several stretcher-bearers were approaching, with their familiar loads.

'It was too good to be true,' said Sara.

'Enjoyed talking to you, Sara. We must do it again.'

An hour later came something Sara had been dreading. A casualty brought in on a stretcher was someone she actually knew. It was Lieutenant Harness, last seen when she was with Johnny in Groppi's restaurant. The officer's left foot was a complete write-off. It was the end of his war but not, she thought, anything life-threatening, and she told him so. For the first time they were very formal together. She called him 'Sir'

151

and she was 'Nurse Cox'. He was in pain, of course, but he was mostly despondent. He talked of how he'd done 'bugger all' except training for three years, 'and now this'. 'What a waste,' he raged. Sara realised that until his wound occurred, the man had been enjoying the fray. She thought – 'That's the professional soldier for you.' It was beyond her understanding. He lay there on a stretcher in a sandy spot, waiting for a berth on a meat-wagon. An army man came along to take away his pistol and ammunition, and the grenades. He looked a sad case, but she'd no time to feel sorry for him. He was a statistic amongst – what was it Wragg had said? – 200,000 men.

Lieutenant Harness was injured on the fourth day of the battle and it was one of the few landmarks in Sara's war. Working on with the same companions she lost track of the days. Curiously enough her physical condition improved. It was never easy, and her back ached deplorably from bending over wounded men, but she found relief in a sort of second wind. She supposed her body was toughening up; what she'd thought of as fitness had been a half-way stage. Even so she slept for every minute allowed to her. She thought that after the battle – if there ever was an 'after' – she could bed down for a week.

Wragg kept her posted on the state of the battle, in so far as he could surmise it. She listened intently to any information about tanks. She shrank from a phrase he used – 'This will be the last great military tank battle' – and hoped that Johnny's sergeant was keeping his crew safe. She took heart from Wragg's description of Italian tanks as 'self-propelled coffins'.

The other event that stuck in her mind concerned Rommel.

The field commander of the Axis forces had died of a heart attack, and Rommel had left his sick bed to fly back to north Africa. That was on the first day in November – in other words the ninth day since the start of the battle.

At last, after twelve days of fighting, came news from Wragg – how did he get hold of this stuff? – that British tanks had made a final thrust and broken through the Axis lines; that Rommel's force was in retreat and the battle of Alamein was effectively over. Instead of relief, Sara felt nothing at all.

There were still casualties, of course, but the numbers diminished. Sara was talking to Wragg during one of the lulls they now enjoyed, when Johnny was brought in on a stretcher. She had known this was going to happen. All those hopes, expressed to herself throughout the conflict, were a sham because she'd known all along. She'd even imagined him being brought to her Regimental Aid Post, though there were long odds against it. Her involuntary cry of 'Oh no!' alerted Wragg, but that too was sham.

The moment she saw him she knew Johnny was going to die. This was strange, because his expression was animated, his tone of voice almost chirpy. She'd seen a kitten run over once, and the creature had made a last frantic dash on wonky legs before lying still.

'I thought – it can't be,' Johnny cried out. 'It can't be Sara. What are the odds?'

'Long odds,' she said, managing to speak at the third attempt. 'So your sergeant...what was his name?'

'George.'

'Yes of course, George. He didn't manage to keep you out of trouble after all.'

'He did his best, old George. Course, we brewed up, didn't we. Had to happen. He got his crew out all right – a bit knocked up, some of us – but George didn't make it.'

Wragg stepped up close to Sara and muttered in her ear. 'I'll look after the others. If there's anything I can do...'

She thanked him.

'I don't think they knew I was frightened,' Johnny said.

'I'm sure they didn't, Johnny.'

'It's a funny thing, this battle,' he went on. 'Once it started we lived the life of Riley. Right before the attack they gave us loads of grub. And airmail cards, as many as you wanted. There's one on its way to you.'

'Thank you, Johnny.'

He was talking ten to the dozen, more than she'd ever known. 'Then some blokes drove up with Thermos flasks of rum and hot cocoa,' he continued. 'Never had rum before. Feel a bit weird, actually.'

'Drunk on parade, Johnny.'

'Trouble is those Kraut Mark IV tanks. They're something else. George hit 'em with a load of 2-pounders. They just bounced off. When we got hit, the old tank was glowing like a light bulb. White hot.' He stiffened for the first time and showed signs of discomfort. 'Know what? What the lads do is have a cigarette.'

'Are you a smoker, Johnny?'

'Never touch 'em. But still...special occasion, eh?'

Sara looked around her, stupidly, because she knew they'd run out of fags long before. She started cursing, but there was an intervention from a man lying nearby waiting for the meat-wagon. He'd given Sara a hard time, refused to co-operate, called her a slag. Now he turned awkwardly on his stretcher and threw across a pack of Woodbines, followed by matches.

'E can 'ave one of mine,' he told her.

She took out a Woodbine and put it between her cousin's lips. 'Keep still, Johnny. Let me light it.'

The match flared, and there was a suggestion of smoke from the end of the fag.

'It's a funny thing,' Johnny said, and closed his eyes. She knew he was dead.

After that Wragg was tremendously kind to her. He sorted out the official details about Johnny's body, then came back to Sara and found her a cup of tea. He'd have arranged for her to go back to the rest tent, but she wanted to keep working. Anything to keep thought at bay. As luck would have it these were more or less the final moments of the battle. Now there

155

was little for any of them to do. Wragg fashioned a crude seat from an old packing case and she sat watching the dregs from 12 days of slaughter. She didn't cry. She didn't think of Karim or Gina or her mother. Around her was the landscape they'd helped to devastate – a burnt-out lorry, the remains of a food dump, bandages and medical detritus, bits of paper blown about in the breeze. The area filled up with men from different units, who sank silently to the ground immersed in their own thoughts. A unit of pipers arrived and their pipe major went up on higher ground and played 'Flowers of the forest'. Finally she wept.

THE END

SOURCES

Below are the main sources used for 'Desert war nurse'.

Penny Starns. *Blitz hospital: True stories of nursing in wartime London.* The History Press, 2018

Good information on the working conditions of hospital nurses during WW2.

Nicola Tyrer. *Sisters in arms: British Army nurses tell their story.* Weidenfeld & Nicolson, 2008

A rare book on QA nurses, including practical medical information and a chapter on North Africa.

Artemis Cooper. *Cairo in the war 1939-45.* John Murray, 1989. Pb edition 2013.

Contains much on the war, but also intensive information on all aspects of social life in Cairo.

Julian Thompson. *Desert victory. (Forgotten voices series)* Ebury Press, 2011

Personal testimony from representatives of all ranks involved in the war, especially on el Alamein.

Malcolm James. *Born of the desert: With the SAS in north Africa*. Frontline Books, 1945. Pb edition 2001.

A vivid impression of warfare in the desert.

David Lloyd Owen. *Providence their guide: The long range desert group 1940-45*. Leo Cooper, 1980. Pb edition, 2001.

Correlli Barnett. *The desert generals*. Phoenix 1960 & 1983. Pb edition 1999.

Critical study of the generals involved in the desert war.

Printed in Great Britain
by Amazon